GUILLAUME

A NOVEL

Michael Arno Bender

COPYRIGHT

guillaume

Table of Contents

GUILLAUME

There was a young handsome monk named Guillaume, who lived in a French village called Le Puy-en-Velay. Guillaume lived with his brother Jacques, and Godescalc, an aging abbot. Life was dull, routine even, but all that had changed one evening.

"There are letters from the Pope!" Jacques announced, as he ran into the main room at the monastery.

Indeed, two letters.

From the Pope.

One letter made Godescalc into a bishop. This, of course, turned Godescalc into a bearable fella for the night.

The other letter was only forwarded by the Pope, but it actually came from from Caliph Abd-ar-Rahman III al-Nasir's secretary, stating that he sent letters to the Pope requesting a few persons of good will, intelligence, and a willingness to learn medicine to come to Cordoba, and join other groups of men from other countries, and he will pay the cost of instruction, housing, and food, and a small gratuity, as well to show his country's generosity, and power. And down at the end of the letter were the words: Venir a Andalusia, or Come to Andalusia.

Weeks later, Godescalc called both young men into his room and they both knew something was going on.

"I took the initiative and wrote to the Pope," said Godescalc. "I told him of your going south to further study besides what medical knowledge you and your brother had learned here, and your desire to know more, all this was fine with him except that he forbade you learning surgery."

"When can we go?" asked Guillaume.

The light had just began to descend upon the earth when the men finally got going. They walked from Le Puy, with their poor donkey, through meadows and beside higher hills. All through Languedoc territory, with Burgundy on their left, traveling south with the river Loire on their right and the Valey Mountains rising later, as they crossed the Loire. They followed the valley down towards the Cevennes Mountains on their left and crossing the river Tarn the following day. It was nearly two hundred leagues as the crows fly to the Pyrenees in Catalonia. But they did not walk and drag their asses as the crows fly, and so it took them twenty days to reach the Pyrenees.

In twelve days they reached Nîmes, a large town, and two days later Montpellier near the sea, then Narbonne and Perpignan where there were many Arabs among the crowds. Then they cut southeast through Roussillon and followed the river into the nearby mountains. Passing around Mount Puigmale, they came within sight of Ribas de Fresser.

"Guillaume!" shouted Godescalc. "Come on, quit dithering!"

Guillaume had stopped to look at a flower he hadn't seen before and on another occasion he stopped to look at a plant, getting out his journal for plants he didn't know of and he described them in detail. He looked at the plant touched and felt it, listened to it, tasted and smelled its parts until his description eliminated all other plants except the one he was looking at.

A hawk saw him and squawked. He stumbled on a hidden rock and accidentally startled a number of Spanish Ibex mountain goats with huge horns and heavy coats. The bucardo jumped away, far away, from them, with snorting boars and their piglets.

At each night's lodging there were most vigorous and numerous lice eating on the skins of night sleepers. For days various muscles of their bodies twitched before they finally took off their clothes and washed them in the broken-iced streams and washed their bodies until they seemed to turn blue with the cold and wind.

They came to a single mountain with a huge waterfall flowing down splashing them and walked through lake valleys with the most exquisite floriated flowers along the sides of large ponds and small lakes. Here the way was much slower and colder for there was still snow on the ground and heavy snow up the rising slopes of the mountains at Ribas de Fresser.

In Catalonia they stopped for a night's lodging, and the next day they went on down to Santa Maria de Ripoll. The small village was in a valley where two rivers crossed and sloped downward. The tiny Abbey had a freestanding six-story lookout tower and a bell. The Abbey was rectangular shaped. The eastern end of it was a large curved front piece, which filled out the inner alter. There were other buildings near by, the outside urinals and sheep pens and an enclosed garden with elevated brambles to keep out animals.

Music carried softly up from below on the cold evening breeze. Their sobs were similar to a mass for the dead: filthy, tired, irritated, mealy-mouthed, whining, with abrasions everywhere, kicking the asses in their butts to make them move.

"Oh, Saint Vitus, give me strength," whined Guillaume.

The older man let out a high-pitched squeak, while his brother Jacques said nothing. Half a dozen Mozarabic monks came out of their buildings. Someone looked out a window, went up to them, and took their asses to the animal shed. Then he guided the men inside to hot baths. The monks always had very large kettles in the fireplace, and gave the travelers the most heated luxurious baths with hot soapy water to lather themselves.

Little kittens came sniffing and looking at the guests, and quickly retreated when a bit of water splashed on them. Other men had by this time washed their clothes in warm water and were hanging them up on clothes string put up near the fireplace. The Mozarabs in Catalonia looked at their guests in wonderment. People usually came up to Ripoll from the South, the West, or even from the East. But monks from the North were rare! A few Jewish merchants went around the coast.

At that very moment a Jew riding a horse with a few other horses as pack animals rode by and said: "Peace be upon you, my friends."

He sweetly bowed to them and gestured with his hand.

And the people present replied: "And peace be upon you as well, sir!"

"Why not go by Le Perthus pass, the coastal route?" asked the Mozarabs. "Why come through Tossa Pass?"

This was as far as Guillaume had come before when he ran nearly all the way, getting here in thirteen days. There was so much mud on his face that it was awhile before they recognized him and when they did there were smiling faces all around for they had remembered Guillaume.

These wayfarers stayed nearly a week before turning south again. The men of Santa Maria de Ripoll thought of Guillaume with fondness. They were good people, these Catalans who spoke Latin with a funny accent.

The guests from Languedoc talked late into the evening with their Mozarab monk brothers about church politics, distant wars, the black taint of poisoned wheat and what to do about it, the summer's harvest of food and the beggars who came by asking for a little something. They heard how much each Abbey gave away to the poor and found out about the latest illuminated Bible, as well as the easiest and fastest way to Cordoba and what the Arabs were like.

The Catalans told them to follow the river past Vic Abbey to the large town of Barcelona on the coast, which had been in Christian hands for many years. It was largely unmolested by the Arabs. The Catalans had put out a call for a woman who had talked to Guillaume the last time he was here in Ripoll.

However, Rosalinda, the folk herbalist, a Basque Majus originally from Navarre, already knew intuitively that he was coming and had set out several days ago toward Ripoll. She didn't seem to have a visible means of supporting herself at first glance. Still she liked Guillaume, enjoyed speaking with him even through a translator, and from time to time enjoyed pulling his red beard. He couldn't understand her language, Basque, but one of the Catalans could and translated back and forth for him, laughing so hard hysterically that he could hardly translate. Obviously, she really liked Guillaume and that created a wild atmosphere of lightening around them.

Rosalinda was in her thirties. She had a big bright smile and long black hair flowing over a loose white blouse. Her long legs were showing under her red skirt. She put one of them high up on the church step and her left hand on her hip, while she was talking and using her right one gesturing away madly.

She had brought with her a basket filled with many kinds of mushrooms and a freshly oven-baked loaf of bread.

Rosalinda spoke again and the Mozarabs translated from Basque into Catalan: "Estar tocat del bolet."

Meaning that she thought Guillaume was touched by the mushroom, slightly wacky but cute. And in the middle of the conversation she was trying to get him to purchase some toadstools that she kept pointing at.

"The white ones with a red cap and white dots on top are the best," translated the Catalan monk.

The Mozarabs laughed: "The mushrooms she wants you to buy would make you crazy for some time when you ate them."

Guillaume asked them if they had ever eaten the mushrooms and the Catalans said no, but they had seen animals having done it. So he shook his head making a negative gesture. Rosalinda came up toward Guillaume, who backed up a little. She reached up and quickly pulled his beard, being faster than him. They both laughed, but for completely different reasons.

Grasping both her hands, he pulled them up into his red-haired beard, rubbed her hands in it to let her know that the color of it would not come off.

"Explain to this lady that if I could see myself through her eyes I should probably laugh much heartier than she."

Guillaume bought her bread.

After Ripoll they went south to the town and abbey of Vic, where they met more Catalan monks and stayed for the night. The next morning they continued heading south, following the river.

Upon entering the territory of Barcelona they began seeing farms and ranch houses in the outskirts of town. The closer they got to the city, the more people they saw, traveling people much like themselves. Soon they could smell the Sea, though they couldn't see it yet.

A couple of nobles came by speaking to one another, interrupted by the loud talking of the peasants and the shouts of townspeople. There was the noise of clanking chains being placed on oxen. And one noticed the fresh smell of straw and hay mixed with horseshit.

The Catalans had told them to keep to the Sea road. Now the roads were good all the way to the Arabic town of Tarragona and from there on down to Tortosa, another Arabic location. And at last they would reach Valencia, where they were to take the road to the southwest to Almansa. From there they had to go to Albacete and in a southwestern direction to Ubeda. And lastly from Jaen their way would bring them to Cordoba.

Having checked their route southward they took in Barcelona with all its crowds and shopkeepers, men carrying butchered meat, horses and soldiers in battle gear, wheelwrights, loaders, wagons filled with small firewood logs, all jostling. There were the sounds of chains hooking and unhooking horses and wagons, men shouting orders, sellers and buyers calling for someone to take and others to give.

They headed over to the coast road and turned south towards Tarragona. Halfway there they ran into more and more Arabs.

Suddenly the wind started to roar. Branches of trees flew into the faces of the monks and it became hard going. The donkeys' eyes widened and their ears moved back. The animals jumped with every flying leaf, stiffened with fear. Even the men began to look to the right and left at the dust and debris. Guillaume thought he saw something but couldn't make it out. Jacques became spooked and the Bishop even had to exercise his authority. The roar became louder around them. Then, as suddenly as it started, the winds died down, followed by visions of eternal Hell. A large black hole appeared before them on the ground. Cautiously they went up to it and tried to stick their toes inside. While doing so they heard a crashing sound, while browned-white teeth like giant walls descended and clenched and started a back and forth motion much like chewing. A pair of white eyes erupted from the hole. Then an upturned nose was visible with hairs sticking

17

out of it. Strange ears emerged and frightened them badly, making them jump back on the top of the foreground. What they saw looked like horns and a mouth spitting out the bones of men.

"The Devil's Den!" said Guillaume.

Out of the mouth came sounds and blood and spittle, which caused them to fall to their knees and finally flat on their stomachs. Dozens of flame-enshrouded strange misshapen looking humpbacked ghouls, with tiny flames were bursting out of them with long tongues flapping back and forth. They were climbing out of the hole towards them, wailing and moaning and high shrieks split the air. They screamed and writhed scratching the ground in front of them. Their asses started, heehawing, some stopped, and others ran away from the strange movements of two of the three men.

From the hill a hundred yards away came the most insane laughter of three or four Arabs who had been watching this activity. These mounted frontier-guards had been watching the men for a long time, looking on the monks whom they at first thought were spies. But upon seeing the monks and their invisible jinn it seemed to them that they were newcomers to the mountains and coast.

"Just a bunch of dumb swine-eaters, looking as if they had gotten a touch of the evil eye," one of them said.

The monks were unknowingly entertaining the bored Arabs for all they saw was the same unremitting landscape all day, every day.

"The Apocalypse," cried Guillaume, seeing snakes coming out of the pit.

And then Jacques also panicked, saying: "The end of times."

The older man was startled and stepped back several paces, shaking his head.

"No, no, it's not the Apocalypse, you idiots!" he said.

And suddenly as he said it, the thing rose up, swirled in the air and spun away.

"It's all in your overworked imagination, come on damn it, get up," he said, and kicked the younger man.

The Arabs came down the hill, walked over and greeted them with huge smiles on their faces. They began speaking in Catalan. As the monks were brushing themselves off, they spoke in Latin at which the Arabs also began speaking in perfect Latin, thanking them for their little entertainment.

"Your Jinn are most realistic," said the first Arab.

"Almost as good as ours," said the second in almost flawless Latin.

"And we wish to thank you all for a most pleasant experience," said the next.

"Where are you going?" asked the last Arab.

"We are going to Cordoba along the south road to Valencia and then cutting off southwest toward the City," said Jacques.

By this time the monks had calmed down, but the Arabs were still smiling and smirking.

One of the Arabs said: "So unexpected."

"So unrehearsed!" said another.

And a third one of them burst out in laughter.

By this time the monks had recovered themselves they were feeling a bit embarrassed, even sheepish. At the same time they were relieved that the Arab border guards were not going to assault them, or at least not steal from them either. They showed them their safe-conduct pass, which the Arabs saw and acknowledged. Then they bid the Arabs goodbye.

"May Allah be with you," said one of the Arabs.

"And may God be with you in the hereafter," said Godesalc.

The castle overlooked them on the mountain. They were now in Saracen territory, in lands that had often been disputed, and they headed south along the sea route to Valencia.

"It is not the demons on you but in you, which you will have to contend with boys. And you are going to have to grow up fast," intoned the Bishop. "St. Roch protect me against the plague."

"St. Lucy protect my eyes," prayed Jacques.

"St. Fiacre protect me against haemorrhoids," laughed Godesalc.

"St. Apollonia protect my teeth," said Guillaume.

"St. Blaise protect my throat," begged Jacques.

"St. Anthony protect me against leprosy," added Godescalc.

They went on now in renewed vigor. Guillaume began to get hungry and pinched off some bread from the loaf Rosalinda had given him, putting it into his mouth to ward off the hunger, chewing it slowly. And within an hour or so he started to feel a bit strange, yet still continued walking.

Jacques was talking about the Arabs and Guillaume smelled his words as if they were Jasmine. But he said nothing and simply continued walking along the road, looking around and tasting all the colors and every shape he could see. Suddenly music went through him. First he heard a small choir, as he was used to and then large melodious choirs coming with loudness. Then it went soft, followed by dozens of choirs. Some were singing before and after one another on separate lines, sometimes several. This was the music he had dreamed of before, but never had heard previously. It was a glorious pulsating music, colored in glowing red, vermilion, viridian, burnt sienna and umber, indigo blue, and yellow ochre. All the colors were swirling and bursting with light. It was something only he could hear and personally feel. Every step he took set off glowing puddles of light, which opened up illuminated rings. They went on and on and on and further and further out in thunderous waves.

Jacques came up to Guillaume and asked: "Are you all right?"

Guillaume had slowed down from his strong strides and became a bit wobbly.

"Umm, yeah, I feel fine," he said, "and how are you?"

"Oh, I'm alright too," replied Jacques.

"Let us stop here for a while and I can rest a little," the Bishop said tiredly.

Guillaume mumbled, "Yes, why not?"

They took off their packs, tied up the donkeys and went looking for wood. Putting the wood on the side of the road got themselves out of the path of on-coming foot, ass, and horse traffic. Then Jacques cut some fine threads of wood and built a nest of shavings with twigs on top and the Bishop started striking the flint stone. Guillaume put stones around the fire and watched the proceedings closely and thoughtfully, while the fire got stronger and stronger.

They took out their wine skins and drank warmed up water. It tasted to them magnificently fine. A few travelers came by.

"How far is Tarragona?" asked one of them.

"It's not far now, another day and you will be there."

The men nodded their thanks.

It was getting late, so they decided to camp here for the night. It was too far from a Saracen tavern and stock house and too late to go back.

The next morning they got up early, shook off their weary traveler's aches and muscle cramps and stretched pulled tendons. Then they began to break camp. The morning's birds were flying and drifting in circles above them and squirrels chatted in what they thought was bird language from the forest nearby, as they walked along the road.

"Yes, your most high and exalted most thoughtful highness, we are so sorry we did not inform your elevated self, Sir, that we were coming!" said Jacques in good spirits to the squirrels.

They moved off and down the road making good progress. By nightfall they arrived in Tortosa, under Muslim rule. The travelers selected a tavern with clean rooms and a stable with good straw for their animals. They could no longer hear the sea as its lapping waves splashed up and washed the glistening sands and jeweled pebbles on the seashore. Tortosa was a little inward from the Mediterranean Sea. Still it was a port town and their dockyards were famous. In the higher mountains stood Suda citadel, as well as a garrison and prison.

The next morning they remarked on how clean and tidy the room was and heated too, it must have been the steam from below. The stable was comfortable and the asses were fed! The monks wasted little time walking around town and went on with their traveling.

Four days later in the afternoon they finally had Valencia in view. They picked the first inn and stable they could find that day. It was a second rate one, but they were so tired that they didn't care.

The following morning rather early they walked around the city and wondered what all the men with carts were doing at this early time of day, picking up all the horse and ass dung and sweeping the streets. A nearby load of dung was being sorted out and mixed in with the soil. They didn't have the faintest idea why this was done, coming from the North with topsoil two feet thick.

They watched the little canals delivering water to the fields and marveled how the Arabs could figure out who had which patch of ground and when would it be watered? And what were those two wheels? One was horizontal, the other vertical, doing turning.

"Oh, yes, now I see the water comes up from below and washes the other wheel," said Guillaume, who was staring at the ditches and wooden mechanical marvels.

"Come on, we'll look at it when we come back," suggested Jacques.

A Mozarab overheard them speaking in Latin, came over and introduced himself.

"You know," he said, "Valencia is called the scent-bottle of Andalusia. There are so many orchards here and flower gardens, with the sweet exhalations of which the air is always heavy."

After Valencia they continued for a day, then they curved to their right in a westerly direction toward Almánsa and on to the larger city of Albacete. From there the route turned more or less southwest to Ubeda, which took them several days, and down to Jaen. At last they went west to Cordoba.

"Would like some bread?" Guillaume asked Jacques.

"Oh, I'd love some, thanks."

They kept walking for some time. Then Jacques began skipping like they did as children, and the Bishop looked and wondered about it. But Guillaume knew where Jacques was coming from and guffawed-coughed to suppress it. And he resisted smiling by puckering up and biting his lower lip in an effort to keep their secret from the Bishop.

Presently, Jacques quietened down and began walking without stumbling again.

"The hills are far," he croaked, "we shall have to have a serious talk with that lady when we see her again."

Guillaume said: "Yes".

The Bishop was about to ask a question, but at the last moment decided not to. Neither Jacques nor Guillaume wanted to talk about it as speaking seemed to destroy the experience. They walked on.

For several more days they traveled down a road, on both sides with mountains, passing through a long valley. They encountered more and more Arabs, some were in quite a hurry. Others crossed their way, going in the opposite direction. It was now well into March and more than two months had passed from the time they left the Abbey, where they spent their childhood's days.

Guillaume saw a new plant, one that he had not seen before and got out his journal and sketched it. He felt its leaves and stem, listened to it, tasted the bitterness of its flower, and smelled its peculiar scent. Afterward he hurried to catch up to his partners with his asses heehawing all the way down the road.

The bishop wanted again to set up camp near the road, but the younger monks said pointed at an inn a few leagues away, just down the road from them. Their eyesight was much better than Godescalc's. So it was decided to rest their bones in a bed of newly mowed straw rather than out here in the wilderness. They were now in a Mediterranean climate, closer to the equator than before and therefore in much warmer weather.

The rather large inn turned out to be even more comfortable than the last one they slept in. Many different kinds of food were available: Jewish, Muslim, and Christian. They were inclined to stay there for a while, as they met quite a few lodgers all speaking different languages.

Suddenly an Arabic troop of horse cavalry galloped up, looking to water their horses and then they took off again. Last year the Muslims had suffered a defeat at the hands of the Christians and still weren't too amused about it. These and other tidbits of conversation Godescalc gathered up as he ordered their meals.

The three Christians turned around and started talking again.

"Yes, this inn is the best we've been in since we came from home," said Guillaume.

"Yeah, it is," remarked Jacques.

"And I'll be glad when I'm home again," intoned the Bishop, which wasn't quite true as this was an investment he'd made with God and Pope, bringing the "boys" down to Cordoba. Actually, he'd wanted to do some traveling himself, besides his yearly journey to Santiago de Compostela. Although this was looking to be the best and newest landscape viewing he had had, this was also the last time he would be coming to the land of the Vandals. His only worry now was that he wasn't quite sure if he'd done the correct thing in bringing the boys here in the first place. These questions had been nagging at the back of his mind since before the first of the year. How would the people at his Abbey feel about his two star pupils having learned Saracens ways and medicine, what would the people think? Would they be thought of as magicians, sorcerers or wizards? Would the people of Le Puy become suspicious and not come to the Abbey anymore? Oh, he thought, we can't have that. He would be in the unfortunate position of having to protect and defend them continuously. What distractions would that entail? It might start a ruckus and begin spreading the word that he encouraged necromancers in his fold.

"Oh, heavenly Father spare me from mine own faults, which I bring down upon myself and have none to blame but myself! Oh, joy!" he said out loud without thinking and in a fit of exasperation, "Oh, Jesus!"

Guillaume and Jacques looked up at him.

"What?" they remarked together.

"Oh, nothing," the Bishop whispered.

He didn't want to spoil their new experiences, so he said nothing.

THE CITY

After walking for some more days, the men reached Ubeda, and then walked to Jaen. And two and a half days later, they camped in the evening outside of Cordoba, just a few hills away. From the position the lights and afterglow were visible of the White City.

In the early hours of the morning they could see the outskirts of the City and smell the orange blossoms. They saw the horse farms, stucco white houses, and people moving around. There were fields of Spanish lavender row on row, all purpled flowers and everywhere different sorts of fine mature trees, vegetable gardens and also ornamentals. Somewhere else they noticed layers of saffron picked by hundreds of people, who were pulling out the tiny stems. And there were beautiful horses.

"How beautiful!" exclaimed Guillaume.

"Supremely so," chimed Jacques.

"You boys have your heads in the clouds," countered Godescalc.

The bishop again looked at his papers, real paper, feeling it, turning it over and over with his fingers. Then he read the instructions within Cordoba.

"Street of Travelers or Traveler's Street, I think," said Godescalc. "We are to see the diplomat Rabi, a bishop or Racemundus, or Raimundo, of Cordoba, whomever he is, and I am supposed to turn you both over to him, sounds to me like a Mozarabic name."

"And we are to seek out a funduq, a hotel for travelers and lodgings for the needy."

The bishop went asking for the directions to Travelers Street, but no one it seemed could understand Latin. Eventually they found someone who understood his language and got the correct directions. The hostel was a very large house with a series of apartments, which all looked alike and ran up to three stories with two patios facing away from the heat of the midday's sun. They went into the officer's apartment and identified themselves.

"Oh, yes," said the administrator, "I've been expecting you for about a week now. Was your journey here difficult? What troubles did you encounter?"

"Allahu akbar allâhu akbar

ash-hadu al lââ ilâha ilia-llâh

ash-hadu anna muḥammadan rasûlu-llâh

ẖayya 'ala-s-ṣalâh

ẖayya 'ala-l-falâẖ

Allâhu akbar, allâhu akbar

lââ ilâha illa-llâh."

"What was that?" asked Godescalc.

"That was the muezzin's melodious voice calling people to prayer. Do you see the minaret over there, next to the Great Mosque?" said the administrator. "Five times a day someone climbs the minaret and recites the adhan."

Godescalc and the administrator talked quietly for a while and then the latter asked a boy to take them up to apartment number 9 and help them get settled in.

While they were doing that the administrator wrote up detailed records on their whereabouts to his superior, including information about their encounter with the Arab frontier guards. He as well included the direction in which they came. This report was sent to the Chief Postmaster: the Caliph's senior spy, who always questioned everyone entering and leaving the territory of Andalusia. He had other people help him with this.

Of course everyone always took him to be the Chief Postmaster, who in a friendly manner simply asked how such-and-such persons were doing, inquiring about the mode of travel, what their business was and how far they were going and when could he expect to see him back in "his" territory with who and how. And if they were important he would have someone waiting for them to help in whatever way they might need if necessary. His helpfulness always tended to make a good impression of Andalusia on foreigners coming from the Eastern part of the Islamic world, or wherever they might hail from.

These people were not doing this because they were paranoid. They merely carried out their duties to keep track of economics, possible warfare, the shipping lanes, to get and keep a sense of the trade. How much, for example, was the price of copper in Al-Hind or India, or the price of ginseng in Al-Sin or China. And was the physician able to bring back to Andalusia in his saddlebags books in which he had secretly put the seeds of sweet oranges or limes? For some reason the government of that territory he acquired them from didn't want to have their seeds exported.

An intelligent man who knew his business could come up with a fairly accurate and detailed "map" of what was going on in the world. Who was doing what to whom and why, and when and where he was going to do it. He knew the Caliph of Baghdad picked his nose in private. More importantly he knew what was on the caliph's mind, in private, at this very moment or, at least he could make you think he knew. He knew that the Caliph of Baghdad was becoming somewhat envious of the Caliph of Andalusia and would in time try to stir up restlessness amongst his people in Abd-ar-Rahman III's conquered territory in North Africa, known as the Maghreb. The desert Sinhaja nomads, who lived there and here in Andalusia were beginning to ferment trouble. These Berbers, lovers of the shifting sands in the desert, were being recruited.

Once a month in peacetime he wrote up his documents in which he teased out some insignificant, fragmented piece of information to present to the Caliph. Of course, all the other monarchs of all countries were more or less doing the same thing. There wasn't anything new there. What was new was the fact that the Chief Postmaster was invisible as the Chief

Spymaster and that spying went on all the time.

Unlike some monarchs, he did not wish to alarm the public unnecessarily. Exposing them to fear or alarm while he grabbed more power for himself was not his way of doing things as he already had all the power he needed or wanted. Even if he had not been Caliph this man would not have seized power, it was not in his character or nature to do such a thing for once having done so the public saw it and some of them too would grab for power. And all the things he had done for Andalusia would have come undone, and fallen away. In short, the Caliph was not a megalomaniac. Nor were most of the men in power. Not even most of the extremely wealthy men of the land, for they would give everything they had away either to the Caliph or to someone they thought worthy on a moment's notice. Such was the generosity of the Arab.

The Caliph was a man of whom it was said that when his ancestors were driven out of power in the East and he had come to this unconquered land. They instilled in their children that it was the land and people giving them all it had and it was their responsibility to give back to them all the energy, and intelligence they had. The

Caliph hoped that all he did in life would make this understanding as clear as he could. He had done that and had unified the land of Andalusia, fighting in numerous wars and for that reason he could say without pride or bitterness entering in to it that, he has had as little as two weeks to himself in all the years he had been Caliph. His reign lasted 49 years. And the shifting sands made way for new men.

He did not favor the rich over the poor, but when he was given a great deal of land from some rich man he thanked him for his support and gave it away to the needy. Everyone's duty was to help out everyone else. This was part of what kept the society of people together. Such was the Caliph's stature as a statesman that the land was at peace for many years.

The Caliph was also an intensely curious man, hence the Spymaster. But what was going in and on the land was not the only thing on this man's mind. He collected books from everywhere and when he had time, which wasn't often, he read them. His only vice, perhaps, that he could be reprimanded for was in his building projects: having once put gold and silver roof tailings on his Government-palace and in being rebuked about it by the head qadi.

His son, Al-Hakam remarked that he ought to have the qadi removed from his position, but his father said he would rather disinherit his son than to get rid of the qadi.

Abd ar-Rahman was interested in medicine. The Caliph had been given a book, a very rare and important one from the Byzantine Emperor, Constantine VII, as a gift for the success of Abd-ar-Rahman's declared caliphate. The book was by the author Pedanius Dioscorides, written in Greek. He had been a physician in the Roman army in the first century. This book was about plants and drugs. The Greek language of the men who were studying it was not as strong as necessary nor as understandable, this special group of men had to ask the Byzantine Emperor for someone who intimately knew scientific Greek. The Emperor sent them a Greek monk named Nickolas.

Rabi was his nickname and the bishop called him that. They talked court politics and what life was like in countries such as Germania and Byzantium, as well as over here in Andalusia. And after listening, Rabi politely inquired with Godescalc, if the bishop didn't want a post in the Caliph's civil administration? Rabi said that he could arrange it. But Godescalc courteously declined saying he would have to get back soon and supervise the building of the Cathedral and finish the Abbey.

They talked about the boys, their aspirations and hopes of becoming doctors and what prospects they would have.

Rabi said it was generous of Godescalc letting his two young men study somewhere else.

"You know," said Godescalc, "you are a very good man and I hope to meet up with you again. Please come up to visit Le Puy some day."

They shook hands on it.

"Before you leave," Rabi said, "you must come to the Government House and palace and let me treat you in style to a fine afternoon's lunch and walk about the place. It is called Madinat Al-Zahra, the city of Zahra, and it's about five leagues northwest of Cordoba. Before you go, have the Administrator of Accommodations send me a note and I'll arrange a horse or litter for you to come there."

"As you wish," replied Godescalc.

And he went back to the hostel finding the boys gone, but with a note saying they were going for something to eat and would be back shortly. So the old Bishop took off his clothes and retired to bed, where he slept like an angel.

The next morning they all woke up together and the Bishop inquired about their night off.

"He had a drink last night," said Guillaume.

"It was called the Liqueur of the Pomegranate and it made all the girls look beautiful, and the City's heavy scent of orange-blossoms," said Jacques.

Until that very evening he had never smelled orange blossoms.

"I can't trust you boys for a moment, can I?" said the Bishop. "Look at yourselves, dissipation and wantonness, written all over you. Are you sure you're monks?"

"Well," said Jacques, "we went down to this place they call the bazaar with the hawi, cuckolds, procuresses, hashish eaters and the amulet sellers. It is where all the food and materials, which everyone makes or brings in from outside Cordoba, are displayed. It was an assault on your senses as they are drowned in smells and scents, your eyes tear up on the distractions you see. And your ears, your ears are beaten by loud sounds of every description. People try and get closer to you than you're used to, as though they are saying come on this way, looking you in the eye, looking at you as if you were a strange beast with five legs and a tail. Their eyes follow you everywhere."

"Suddenly you've become a captured man, a victim, but you don't care, all you need do is fill your being with little temptations, a little won't hurt and you tell yourself the food is so cheap," added Guillaume.

The men laughed.

"The shopkeeper will tell you his life story and his wife will tell hers and the children will give you little drinks of something called tea," continued Jacques. "Here you are expected to bargain and not pay the first price.

"We strolled by the carpet makers," said Guillaume, "where these wooden shuttles rapidly fanned back and forth making the most exquisite carpets you have ever seen, soft. There were jewelry shops and the music came from everywhere. We were interested in their herbal medicines of every kind and for every illness a quick cure or two or three. The whole thing was a bit mind-boggling.

There was a kind of magic here that we never see in the North. They have a way of cooling off their shops. I am not sure how the mechanism works, but it does. There were men with perfume from vials around their necks, and glassblowers who make anything on demand! There were swords of Damascus and Toledo, tile makers, potters, lute makers, and musicians, as well as fortune tellers, faith healers, snake-charmers, and women doing tattoos with henna."

"Not to forget the men who sold traditional herbal medicine and those who had something called Baraka," interrupted Jacques. "And men with trained snakes and water sellers with their brass cups doused in rose water and orange-blossoms. They wear large funny looking colored hats with red and yellow tassels hanging down and tiny bells ringing!"

"We went to a stand with drinks," said Guillaume. "We had a wonderful drink iced with snow from the mountains, called the liquor of the Pomegranate."

"Ladies and young women of all ages with their faces uncovered came by us looking at our clothes and putting their fingers up to their nose rubbed it," Jacques continued. "I wondered what they meant?

After the drink I thought all the young women were surpassingly beautiful. But then, I haven't seen that many women. And we had to leave, the bazaar was so overwhelming, I was drunk on it and the liquor."

"I staggered back to the hostel," exclaimed Guillaume. "And it did seem as though everyone was there including quacks, magicians, acrobats, fortune tellers, men who ate flames, of course, you were simply distracted from God, there was no doubt, saddle-makers, harness-makers, all the things you would need for a horse were made there, including tents, little bells for camels and yes they sold those strange looking animals called camels, too!"

Jacques continually said: "It was as if I were dreaming a dream, or moving in a dream and such was our introduction into Arabic."

Then Jacques fell silent.

"Ah huh," shouted Godescalc, "and now that you've tasted hell, would you like to wallow in it?"

"I would not like to wallow in the fountain outside as it is meant for drinking not bathing or washing one's clothes in," said Jacques.

"What?" asked the bishop. "You didn't try to wash your clothes in the fountain, did you?"

"I got my winter cloak about half-washed before the Administrator came rushing out of his office screaming and yelling at me as if I were some country-bumpkin," said Guillaume. "Telling me that the wash basins were in the back of the apartments, this was drinking water and that the baths for washing ourselves were all over the City, and then he said he was sorry he hadn't told one of us earlier. And furthermore the water for the horses and donkeys was in front of the apartments, while the drinking water for people was in the fountains."

"Well," said Godescalc, "it looks as though we all have something to learn."

Before the week was gone, Rabi had sent a litter for the bishop and all three of them were with difficulty packed into it. The bishop wanted the boys not to miss this opportunity to see Government House, none had ever been in a litter before and they found it very different from riding donkeys or walking.

Here they could see that the grates were carefully chosen and close together so the horse's hooves could not penetrate them. There were unlit street lamps and they had time to look around at the trees and the people going about their business.

The sewers were all under ground with iron grates over them, the iron bars being something very new to them. Everything was so whitely painted with geraniums in little flowerpots, decorating the sides of buildings. And there were different iron grates outside wooden windows with their levers, which could be lifted or pushed down depending on the height of the sun. Now that they looked up they saw different sized pots here and there on white walls in the city of orange-blossoms.

The beautiful carvings on the windows were all the same, but on different buildings there were different ones and sometimes mosaic tiles could be found on lovely fountains. They were unable to see people's homes, as they did not front on the streets, but were set back within walls and garden shrubs with front iron gates or carved panels and wonderfully carved and heavy bronze door knockers.

Their color schemes seemed different as well, for they often had exclusively white buildings, but with different colored front entrances and sometimes bricked sidewalks. There was always something to break up the whiteness.

Then they were out in the country, going at a high rate of speed. In a few minutes they found themselves in the middle of a procession of marble columns with mules tugging away at them on wheeled platforms. Hundreds of men were moving along the congested road when finally they all got to the entrance of Government House and palace.

They got out and thanked the man who told them to go through the curtains. Someone else would guide them to their "department of state" and someone would take them to Rabi.

At last they came upon his office and there he was writing something to someone, and greeting them with his smile.

"Well, there you are and I gather you found us alright," he said. "But first, as it's so early I'd like to take you to the Villa of the Water Wheels and show you what our wealth is based on, you see, what makes the whole thing work."

The litter came round the entrance and as they admired the wonderfully well-kept gardens, they thought this in itself was enough to see. Then his horse came with a rider and he got on motioning them to follow and off they went.

Within a few minutes they came to a villa of an extremely wealthy man, a man of such high caliber as to be more of a royal retreat. His villa was placed in the midst of an exotic, fabulous garden and an aviary of rare birds.

Rabi began explaining: "You see, everything is based on water, excellent soil, and fertilizer. We have some means of controlling the water in this region by the use of hydraulic wheels and by putting one of them in the river wherein the river drives the wheel, lifts up the water and discharges it in an irrigation canal. This wheel is made entirely of wood. There are no gears. You see over there is another usually smaller wheel set on its side, turned by a donkey. And this wheel moves round and round onto another vertical wheel with a toothed rim and with a chain link system, bringing water to the surface and dumping it into an irrigation canal by the pot garland wheel. Incidentally, on the other wheel, called a Noria, a farmer can use the water now or wait until the dry season has dried up all the water and then slowly begin to allow the water out of a tank or dam and it will go toward watering dry fields. There are also underground canals around here in places where there was no other way to irrigate and some of them actually have been drilled through solid rock. You see, water is more precious than blood, for blood can be had at anytime but not water. You know, of course, that the mechanism for getting water down from the mountain, which goes by streams, is also managed by men who are called Levelers. These men design and lay out just where the water goes. If it goes down the mountain too quickly then there are little walls dividing the water flow, so that it may go to different people or into holding tanks if the farmers are not ready for it."

The men from the North listened with fascination.

"And," continued Rabi, "one can't steal their designs as they are all different. For example, your situation in the North would not fit any of the water- design ways they have here. You have way too much water and these people never have enough and so it must be released a little at a time. The problems have been studied in depth and they know without a doubt just how much water a plant needs, how much a field with vegetables needs and when it needs it. All these are simply parts of a system; the farmer takes the best seeds for plants and plants them at the correct time of year based on the work of the best calendars. I am writing one now, entitled 'The Calendar of Cordoba'."

All this was totally new to the northern monks.

"The water agents begin letting the water out from the dam," said Rabi, "or down from the mountains at a correct time and the farmers one by one open the little doors or turnstiles in the fields to let it flow to each man's field equally, depending on the size of his field, and whether it was vegetables or spices growing there. Sometimes in this climate it gives three or four crops a year and there is the fertilizer constantly put on and mixed in the soil. As a matter of fact there are different fertilizers for different soils. And even this is not the end, for each year is slightly different from the year before, needing more or less water. The Roman engineers were good but the Muslims are much better, for the Romans did not grow up and live in the desert! They got much of their knowledge from the Persians and the Arabs got much of their knowledge from the Nabataeans. Now let us go back to the palace for lunch."

The purple-red silk curtains in front of the salon hall blew gently in a light breeze as they pulled up. The garden had not yet been planted, but the great bulk of stonework had now been finished. He turned his head to the right and saw the nearly built congregational mosque.

The men walked on through the palace in which the finish work was being done and continued into the other parts of Government House. The effect of the marble floors was cooling, especially when shoes and sandals were taken off and their bare feet were directly touching the floor. The building was facing a direction to let the wind through, which contributed for a cooler interior. Rabi led the way to the huge dining room where nearly everybody came to eat.

"How many people live here?" asked Jacques.

"Oh," answered Rabi "around 7.000, I think. Around 1.000 loaves of bread are made daily just to feed the fish in the ornamental ponds!"

"This place is vastly larger than I could imagine," said Guillaume.

Jacques added: "You know, when you look out into the sunlight and see the marble it looks blue and seems as if you are on a small nearby lake and I am sure that when the gardens are planted it will look fabulous."

"You have no idea just how long and how hard was the work of polishing that marble," said Rabi. "And after lunch we will take a little trip to what somebody has called the rich hall."

"Oh," said Jacques, "there must be hundreds of fountains both inside and outside."

"Several thousand. Actually 3,785 as of last week," said Rabi. "You see, water, again is life, particularly splashing water is music to the ears, and when listening to it, it induces ecstasy. You should have been here in the earlier part of the year when the almond trees were in bloom, forests of them, and the perfume off the trees. It was quite a sight."

A girl brought grapes in a small bowl and placed it on the table. Another girl brought drinks of arrope, which was really rubb, a syrup used as honey and diluted with a bit of water it turned into a wonderful drink. Yet another girl brought olive oil, vinegar and Sevillean figs.

Another dish was rice with saffron, along with three glasses of orange-blossom and rose water were also served. And there was a dish of rabbit with snails and the main dish of Buraniya was served, which Rabi had asked for, tasted and decided it was cooked to his liking. They were all very hungry and delighted in the excellent meal. Dessert was a dish of little cookies with sweets and almonds in them.

After lunch Rabi took them back to town to the Great Mosque of Cordoba. They came upon a huge rectangular building, the largest building they had ever seen. They disembarked with Rabi motioning to take off the shoes and sandals. Then we all walked inside with respect. The first thing that greeted them was red brick alternating with white stone on arches, double arches and on the tops of a forest of jasper pillars. With the greatest amazement they looked around, unable to say anything to anyone.

Rabi walked to a place amongst the red and white stripes on dark-colored jasper and sat down on a small rug. He told us that this is about where we would come for our medical training once our Arabic could withstand the amount of knowledge we would have to learn.

Then he took them outside to the garden of oranges and dates, where the monks had their first sweet oranges. They all simply stood around eating, while watching the water flow through the cement grooves around the orange trees. These sweet oranges were a unique treat! It was beginning to get late, so Rabi bid them well, and said he would check on them from time to time to find out how their Arabic was coming along and how the schooling was going!

BROTHERS

Godescalc spent ten more days with the young monks. Having gotten Jacques alone one day, he asked him to be sure and take good care of Guillaume.

"I will do that," Jacques replied.

And then the bishop got Guillaume aside alone and also asked him if he would take care good care of Jacques? And Guillaume said he would. Having done that, Godescalc said he wanted written reports of everything they did and were planning to do each month. And then he was gone. It was their first time in their lives on their own.

Every morning they both went out gathering plants in the outskirt to learn about the vegetation of Andalusia. They were always asking people about the plants they found and what they knew about them. Then the monks would bring them back to their apartment and put them in clay pots, showing them to physicians they met and asking questions. They were creating a network of communication. The physicians they asked answered their questions in ways they never knew. Gradually these young men were in fact becoming sociable gentlemen.

After a while they had plants and medicinal plants with more in the former than in the latter category. And they also divided their plants between annuals and perennials. The annuals would usually not to survive winter. Even though, the Andalusian winters were more like what the monks considered spring back home.

Every day during the summer and fall they kept gathering plants and asking questions about them, and learning more about them. Their knowledge of Andalusian plants began to grow. Their Arabic also grew and they were communicating in low grade Arabic after six months.

In September, they both contacted Rabi because they thought their Arabic was good enough to start lessons. Rabi wrote back and told them to give it another month. And every day they went out to the bazaar and among all the people, trying out their Arabic, which brought smiles and howls of laughter all around.

In another month they were ready. The young men noticed that everyone including the lowliest had great self-esteem, were proud and individualistic. They could not write Arabic very well at all, but they were beginning to read the language while still making mistakes.

Jacques, his smarter, younger brother was much more fluent than Guillaume. People also laughed when he translated.

Guillaume and Jacques found out that a class was forming in the Great Mosque. Some of the students called it the Cordoban School of Medicine. The chief of physicians and surgeons in Cordoba was a Christian lady who was starting up a new class. These classes had been going on for only a few years. The young men attended that class.

The lady began to speak in a slow manner: "Mohammad, peace be upon him - has explained to us that for every illness there is a cure. The cures and modifications are in these books, and in the heads of many men, the knowledge of which has been built up for centuries by intelligent, hard working, and conscientious men of the Greeks and our Islamic community."

She held up various books.

"Galen, Hippocrates, Al-Razi, who was the greatest physician of our time. And Ex Herbis Femininis, which we think is by Dioscorides, Aristotle's Organon, and Hippocrates' Aphorisms, to mention a few. I do not believe in blind reverence and I hope that you all will not do so either. Here, we all learn from experience, adjusting our knowledge as we go in treating our patients as best we can. Our medicine is based on the Greeks, but it is also based on the medicine of India as well as China. The humeral system is universal. In our education we will learn to understand the Latin way as well. The Commander of the Faithful once had an earache. Whereupon he had a Mozarab physician take a look at it and the man cured it. So we are not averse to using other people's knowledge if it is good. This is a parallel knowledge of medicine besides ours and we respect it."

Guillaume let his attention drift.

The chief of physicians said: "We are not all hidebound traditionalists here, but if any of you wish to challenge Galen's Humeral Theory we would wish to ask you first what you would replace it with? Formerly, when we did not have a school we simply allowed our doctors to study with physicians and learn the profession. And this is still being done. But now, today, we have also started a School besides the way we have always taught and instructed those who would come after us. We want you to be thinking physicians, as well as good memorizers. Some of you are from foreign countries and some of you are doctors, some both. We want you to use your common sense. To meet our high standards you will be instructed to take yearly oral examinations and after the third year you will be awarded the license to practice medicine in Cordoba and its outlying territory. We use the Qur'anic verses, and a Hadith and you will first study the Tibb-an-Nabawi, the Prophetic Medicine. So I welcome you all here and wish you all the success you may earn. Now I shall turn you over to some of your teachers."

The first day, Guillaume and Jacques began learning the relationship between the spirit and the soul and the soul and the body and how all medicine is under the tenets of religion. The method of therapy was outlined that the patients were treated through a scheme, starting with prevention, diet and physiotherapy. If this failed, drugs were used, and at last, surgery would be resorted to, but as a very last resort. The physiotherapy included exercises and hot water baths. It was an elaborate system of dieting and being aware of food deficiencies. Proper nutrition was an important item of treatment.

"And now we begin to learn the humeral system; and behind the humors are qualities such as dry, moist cold and hot. Each of these may be one to four degrees. It can be explained how disease arises as a result of imbalances in these humors. The humors are air, bile, phlegm, and blood. We shall also talk about the importance of diet in a person's health. It should be the first concern of the physician. You will also learn the therapeutic and pharmacological importance of diet, prevention. Not to forget simple and compound medicines, music as medicine, hypnotherapy, aromatherapy, prayer, herbal bathing, baraka, meditation as medicine, spiritual healing, trance-dance, as well as dream interpretation or any combination of the above. We have a good many retired physicians who are eager to work, teach, and help you with your studies. So that you may get the fullest and best training in medicine and pharmacology in Andalusia. If most of you return to your own countries you may find that some of the plants and plant knowledge you bring with you are inadequate for our plants do not grow there. However, with your knowledge and the knowledge of local herbalists, and folk healers, you should not have too much trouble. Or you may have the same plants there as here, but you find they are not of the same strength. Never underestimate your patient's power of belief for it is on his side that it is working as well as your own. The patient wants to get well. We know the patient will feel better and we know today that a patient who feels better is helped by the power of belief in his recovery. Always test your assumptions, some of them might actually be correct."

Most of the students took notes and listened carefully.

"In pharmacology, among the best of us are those who test out their medicines on themselves, or on animals before they begin to prescribe medicines to others. Perhaps you've forgotten a step in the preparation or made a preparation of $1/10^{th}$ the strength, or worst of all prescribed the wrong medicine altogether. And lastly, there are a few books on ethics, responsibilities and liabilities, which you must also study. This is enough for your first day."

Guillaume and Jacques left the mosque very intrigued by what they learned in their first day's lesson. They both knew it was going to be a long, hard time before they became physicians. It was going to be very helpful for Guillaume to have Jacques with him side by side learning from the same texts. Jacques rushed through his work very effortlessly. They each found ways to help one another and this made their studies easier, thorough and complete. One of them understood one thing, but the other might understand the same thing a bit differently. When this happened they exchanged viewpoints. They each gained in the process, something that wouldn't have happened if they were studying alone. As a result of this advantage they more quickly advanced to become top students.

The following day in the Great Mosque they began to learn about plants and the effects they had on people. Then books were handed out and they were told to copy them, or have them copied and handed back in again within several months. It would also improve immensely their Arabic calligraphy.

What really surprised the young men from the North was the fact that these books were written on paper, not parchment, which was made from skin of sheep or goat, or polished vellum, which was made from the skin of a calf. And they slowly began to realize the tremendous technical advance paper had over vellum. It was so much easier and cheaper to make!

According to one of their teachers, the Islamic armies had fought a very successful battle with the Chinese in the 8ᵗʰ century and had captured a few Chinese whose work at home was making paper. As a result of posing a few pointed inquires, paper making came all the way to Andalusia.

In the last twenty-five years or so the Caliph's libraries had been expanding at far faster rates than ever before and now every class in society had paper to use at much less than the cost of parchment.

Guillaume asked: "How many books does this ruler have in his library?"

"I am not sure. Perhaps I think one or two hundred thousand?" the teacher remarked with an uncertain gesture of his shoulders.

Guillaume collapsed on the floor.

"I think he's fainted," exclaimed Jacques.

Some men loved women too much. Guillaume loved books too much. In a minute he came around and got back up on his feet.

They had to keep their voices low as in the Mosque grammar, jurisprudence, recitation of the Qur'an, prophetic traditions and lexicography were taught right along and beside the classes in medicine.

Guillaume remarked whispering: "We only have thirty-seven books and we don't even have a library!"

"Well, we have fifty or sixty libraries around this City and all of them well attended in the evenings," the teacher managed to just rub it in.

He was actually amused.

"I suppose that if you really wanted to, you might, if you went to rural areas, I suppose, you could find an illiterate person, who, however, could compose for you on the spot a rather decent poem or recite a far better one by some of our famous poets in vogue."

"And I suppose," Jacques remarked sarcastically, "that if you went into our rural areas you could probably find thousands of illiterates, who wouldn't know what the hell a poem was."

The teacher changed the subject.

"And if you really wanted to see just how and why we are accomplishing all this, why, there are rooms and rooms filled with people copying all the books we have at the expense of our ruler. He had those who needed to travel east obtain some special books from Baghdad and Damascus and from estate sales. A book with new scientific ideas in it cannot be out for more than a month or two before it has traveled here, copies are made of it and distributed to all the public libraries."

"Our ears are yours," Jacques mumbled.

"Those copied books will be checked for accuracy. It is slightly maddening to walk through these copyist's gardens and listen to all that babbling. The copyists are not only well paid they gain quite an updated education in the bargain. Eventually some of the better ones in four or five years will be in charge of hundreds and some of thousands of young copyists. The copying house business is expanding not arithmetically but geometrically."

Jacques, ever the comedian, stepped in front of Guillaume and closed his mouth. Guillaume gave his brother an annoyed look and stepped on his foot.

That evening in their apartment Guillaume said thoughtfully: "You know, we weren't as cheerful, playful and relaxed up in the North as we've been down here. I think it was because it was so gloomy and so cold in the winters there with having to get up so early for strict prayers. Always for prayers."

"Yes," his brother replied, "here even our rooms are warmed for us."

"Up there we never could let down our spirits and cheer even for a moment for fear we'd have let down our brothers and made fools out of ourselves, but here…"

"And in the summers we were always filthy, dirty with mud up to our backsides doing the most backbreaking work imaginable. I easily remember crawling into bed so tired that I instantly fell asleep and woke with pain. Oh, so much pain. It never left you, not for one whole day and not for an hour. And there was never ever enough to eat."

"Here, our pleasures multiply, a hundred at a time."

"After our graduation we'll probably stay and practice for a time, but then we'll be needed home in Le Puy."

"Yes, if some dumb son-of-a-bitch and his idiotic in-laws doesn't brand us as heretics or magicians, and cause such a stink that the bishop doesn't have us thrown out and cast into the wilderness."

"Oh, I don't think things are going to be as bad as all that," Jacques ruefully remarked. "After all, we needn't say where we'd gone or what we were doing or say anything at all in Arabic, or have anything Arabic with us which might be read as demonic symbols except that we'd studied abroad, I think it will be alright."

"Sure, you're just trying to cheer me up, aren't you?" Guillaume chuckled.

Jacques had gone to the market, sidestepping to avoid some bogus pilgrims and conjurors, to get some eggs. Upon coming home he thoroughly beat them in a bowl until they became like water. He put in some gum Arabic, which he had also bought along with vinegar and honey to vary the consistency.

The gum Arabic was sold in solid lumps and were powdered and dissolved in water. Cheese glue was used with folium; a thin layer of metamorphic rocks was mixed in a separate container.

He had carbon ink for black. Grounded up lapis lazuli made blue or he could make juice from blue flowers, which could be stored in a cloth or clean linen rag moistened with quicklime and a bit of water and dipped in plant juice. Bistre or brown made from burnt resinous wood boiled in lye made a kind of brown and used both as a color and as a shading agent with other pigments. Verdigris or green was made by subjecting strips of copper to the fumes of vinegar, which he had learned in the bazaar. Verdigris was not ground into a powder, but was soaked in wine and thickened by heating.

Media such as gum water, and egg yolk and cherry juice were advised. Malachite, copper carbonate, was common and easy to use as green pigments or they could be extracted from plants and stored in cheesecloth. Vergaut was a mixture of indigo and orpiment. The latter was a native orange to lemon yellow, arsenic trisulfide. For gray a mixture of white lead and black was used. Vermilion was obtained from cinnabar or red lead. White was made with lead and by subjecting plates to vinegar fumes. Wine was used as a medium.

"And," said Jacques, "I bought some real gold leaf and not the yellow paint I've been used to dealing with!"

This was a difficult and time-consuming process for Jacques to get set up for painting. He had gotten a few boards put up as a table on which to work and mix his paints.

Jacques made himself a small collapsible A-frame as an easel, which he placed on the boards positioned against the walls and then he took his ink pens and brushes and began trying them out with the pigments he brought with him. It required some practicing until he could accomplish the same level of competency, which he had up north.

Then he sat quite still for some time designing out in his mind just how he wanted the illuminated page to turn out.

In class next day another man introduced himself, his name was Muhammad Ibn Al-'Udhri and he began telling them about how medicines were made.

"In medicine," he said, "we have different ways of making them from syrups and robs, stomachic confections and electuaries; a medicine composed of drugs mixed with honey or syrup to form a paste, pills and aperients. Or we have a laxative, decoctions and infusions, clysters, enemas, a rectal injection, and suppositories. Tooth powder to rub is used in cleaning teeth. We have gargles to wash or rinse. And confections, which are a sweetened compound of drugs or anything prepared or preserved with sugar. Not to forget preserves, to keep things from rotting. To induce sneezing, we got sternutatives. Eventually you will learn how all these and much more are made, although we are now having pharmacists who know everything about pharmacology and who usually produce medicine themselves. Lastly, the mortar and pestle are your best friends."

The teacher looked intensely at his students.

"Next," he said, "knowledge flows often from many streams. From Sanskrit through both Persian and Arabic into Latin is one stream. From Akkadian through Aramaic, Hebrew, Syrian, Greek into Arabic and now to Latin, is another. Many of these places are either unknown or sound strange to your ears, yet these streams all form a river into Latin and Arabic to you. And that is all I have to tell you today. May Allah's Peace and blessings be upon you."

That evening was warm and smelled of musk and jasmine as the young men went strolling past the Jewish quarter with its narrow streets and high second story patios, the covered walkways with windows on either side, and arches over the streets. There were beautiful balconies with decorative iron railings and bougainvillea entwined around them. And high-filigreed lamps were providing light down on the cobblestone streets, where song and music was floating through the perfumed air.

But the young men could not understand the Ladino language, yet they still appreciated the Jewish melody and continued their walk, strolling on past the market. The evening's cool breezes mixed with the smells of meats braising and vegetables cooking in the night air along with other unfamiliar smells of roasting and fritters cooking. They stopped to get something to eat. Then they walked on toward the Great Mosque, up to the Mozarabic church and went inside to hear the Latin's high pitched voices in Hispanic chanting.

The monks then decided to take in the city's baths, where nakedly they were scrubbed and their spines were adjusted. They were exhausted afterwards, yet they loved the new refreshing smell of their bodies and strolled home to their apartment, where they fell into a very deep sleep. Guillaume dreamt of floating Monasteries placed in giant soap bubbles all alike, slowly twisting and turning on a quiet night's slumber.

The following evening they went the opposite direction down to the weaver's street.

One man was singing:

"Weaver of words, weaver of words,

Come weave me a tale to tell,

Weave me a song to sing, Oh, word weaver.

Weave me a dance to step to, Oh, weaver..."

"See how the design changes with the loom on different singing words, it is as though there is a song woven into the pattern of each of these clothes, carpets and drapes," remarked Jacques.

"Yes," Guillaume interjected, "each change, but with the same design, interesting."

"Let's get something to eat, I'm getting very hungry."

"Yeah, me too. Those textiles are beautiful and gorgeous without compare," said Guillaume.

At last their Arabic was coming along and for the first time he understood the muezzin's call from the minaret:

"God is great! God is great!

I witness that there is no God but God!

I witness that Muhammad is the messenger of God!

Come to the prayer! Come to the prayer!

Come to success! Come to success!

God is Supreme! God is Supreme!

There is no God but God!"

On their way to the food market they passed the jewelry section where many items of gold were made, including earrings.

"Boy, I bet girls would love something like that and did you see those golden necklaces and the pearls all like moonlight white," Jacques exclaimed.

"Well, we aren't permitted girls or women in our order, and even if we could, you don't need to imagine how poor we are. The people who are rich enough to buy these things think nothing of it. And now that we've discovered how poor we are, shall we go home and dream or do we go home and forget about it?" said Guillaume.

In the following days Guillaume and Jacques began to learn diagnostics and they spent months looking at ways to diagnose the many different ailments of the stomach from ulcers to worms; stomach ailments being at the top of the list of diseases and the pathologies of disease or the changes a disease causes in tissues. They also began to learn a little bit about the differences in drugs such as aloes, cassia, saffron, frankincense, myrrh, mastic, pepper, storax and what can be done with ginger, opium semen, coloforia, ciminum, fenogrecum, linum, rock-parsley, pitch, and terebinth. All these drugs were imported from the East.

"We would have to know where to get them, we need to know the exact species, when it was harvested, the exact amount of dosage and frequency and site of administration, the conveyance such as wine or water, the morphology of drug preparation and the correctness of diagnosis," said another physician.

"In the name of Allah, the Compassionate, the Merciful! Praise be to Allah, the Lord of the worlds; and his benediction be upon his messenger Muhammad, peace be upon him, our refuge from perdition," intoned the Arab teacher.

The following day another physician was talking about aromatherapy or the use of incense as practiced by Christians, Jews and Muslims. In Greek-Orthodox churches it was practiced as part of a daily ritual. The most famous was, of course, frankincense, a result of burning the gum resin. Inhaling the fumes was the treatment for epilepsy and regulating of the menstrual cycle, liver illnesses, and stomach pains.

The instructors began talking about the results of aromatherapy in medicine, how the doctors had to understand the patient's mind and to know just when and what kind of incense to use to help alleviate the problems, whether mental or physical.

Another instructor came in and said: "The doctor must know the astrolabe in order to compute the planets if he has had no almanac at hand, and he must know how to cast a horoscope."

Then he showed the students how to tell time with the astrolabe in the day or evening.

When he'd finished he said: "Allah alone knoweth the truth, to Him do we return."

And with this the day's schooling came to an end.

That evening Rabi and another Mozarabic monk named Jawad came to visit Guillaume and Jacques. And Guillaume fascinated Rabi with his progress in Arabic.

"I'm going to leave Jawad with you to help teach you as much Arabic every evening as you can grasp, the yearly examination comes much faster than you suspect," said Rabi getting up, "ma as-salama."

He was waving goodbye to them and suddenly he was gone.

Jawad said: "Let's get started…"

And as each day passed they gained a little more confidence and improved their Arabic. On the weekends they reviewed what they had learned from Jawad, their declensions and conjugations, as well as their etymologies.

The pace continued in class when another instructor was talking about a mineral called amber used in these days medicinally to combat ailments such bleeding and diarrhea. Yellow amber was called the Lantern of Rum, found also in the West of Andalusia along the seashore by digging underground.

"And by the way along our western seashore Arabs found some mollusk, which they called suf al-Bahr, seashell-wool. It got washed ashore at certain times and shed its beard on the rocks of the seashore where craftsmen collected it. It is said it has a golden sheen-like color and a changing hue in different lights. This seashell-wool was so special that only the Caliph and his family can wear it. And I think it is softer than silk."

In the months that followed there was no time for games as Guillaume and Jacques were working twelve hour days on medicine and Arabic, seven days a week. Month after month, they struggled with no let-up. There was no time off and gradually they began to grow up before they grew old, as old Godescalc always said to them. And they grew tired, very tired. But they pushed on.

After their first year they were given oral examinations and both passed well. Guillaume made it to more than three-quarters of the way up and Jacques near the top of the class. And Jawad also gave them an oral and written examination in which both passed fairly well, though both needed somewhat more work and unfortunately both men's writing could do with a great deal of refashioning. Rabi was pleased with the way everything had gone with them and Godescalc in his letters was pleased as well.

Guillaume and Jacques decided to take a little time off to unwind and relax, so they walked over to the edge of the Guadalquivir, Cordoba's great river.

They strolled along for a while, neither saying a word, feeling too dumb to think or say anything, bone tired, and stood on the walkway across the river and watched people coming and going.

Then they continued walking towards the outskirts of Cordoba, past the innumerable mills and Jabal Al-Ward, the mountain of the rose, owing to the rose trees growing there. Their minds were completely numb and everything washed past them in a blur.

Finally Guillaume spoke: "We have to see Rosalinda and talk with her about that drug she gave us, what its good for."

Their plant hunting had to be postponed for their journey and they hired an older boy to water their garden. The plant collection had grown enormous and had helped them in their education on drugs. Not all the drugs were medicinal, nor were all of them perennials and the annuals had begun to die back.

DOCTORS

A days later, the brothers walked over to the Palace and Government House. They went there to talk to Rabi about going for a short trip, as there was a month break from their studies. And in walking they had a chance to see and appreciate more of the landscape and building projects.

Rabi agreed saying: "Go ahead, but you might write Godescalc."

"We already have, and we are going a different way to Ripoll up through Toledo, but we will need some money for the trip and he said to ask you whom he will reimburse upon our completion of our medical studies."

"Ah, how much will you need?" asked Rabi.

The young men hired their asses and piled their equipment on them the same way Godescalc had instructed them and in mid-morning began walking north.

This was the beginning of the farmer's year when all the trees were covered against the frost: the orange, jasmine and lime. Now the quince, pomegranate and peach were ready to eat along with chestnuts, sorb apples, and acorns, all ready for distribution to the cooks to be prepared for dining.

Guillaume and Jacques had learned from a few farmers the healing effects of the celandine and how its flower makes a lotion to soothe the eyes and the juice heals burns. It was always planted in September before the rains came.

The road to Toledo was clear, wide, and well made. When they got close to Toledo and had crossed the Roman Alcantara Bridge, they looked over the Algodor River, while taking the left-hand road parallel to the river. In three days time they were in Toledo. And after another ten days they passed through Zaragoza. Then they got to Ripoll where Rosalinda waited for them laughing her head off with that deep laugh of hers. The Catalan who knew Basque and translated for them wasn't around. After a few days Lliapund came back from Barcelona and began to translate their questions to her.

"What was that drug you gave us in the bread?" asked Guillaume.

"It was the mushroom, you know, a rad cap with white spots on it. A mushroom that flourishes in the shade of certain," she said.

"Does it heal or cure anything?" Guillaume wanted to know.

"Of course," bubbled Rosalinda, "what do you need to cure?"

She burst out laughing. This woman had an ulterior motive up her sleeve for she had trapped them into eating her mushroomed bread instead of the mushrooms she had in her bag and which they didn't want. They weren't quite sure what she was laughing about, but since it was so infectious they couldn't help joining with her without having the faintest idea why they were laughing.

Rosalinda also told them that opium cured the 'holy fire'.

Guillaume was startled and said: "How did you know I was interested in preventing or curing holy fire?"

Back in Cordoba in their classes Jacques thought to himself that his dumber, older brother was going to try again and push his luck all to hell.

"Oh, no, no, no, don't, please," he said to himself.

"Yes," said the teacher.

"Opium cures ergot," stated Guillaume proudly.

"And do you know this for a fact or through heresy?"

"But I would prefer prevention," said Guillaume.

"I asked you once before and now I ask you again, do you know this for a fact or heresy?" asked the teacher.

Guillaume said: "I received the information from a herbalist woman from Navarre and the second part I thought up for myself."

Then he sat down.

"Ladies and gentlemen, this young man has deemed it permissible to say that he knows a way to cure ergot of which he has been told by a woman, for Allah's sake, an herbalist from some place up in the north that opium cures ergot. Does he mention the word observation or has he been told the moon is blue-green? He has also exclaimed and deduced that while people are running around behaving madly, jumping out of second story houses and buildings and others are attempting to drown themselves in their own baths and the rest are running around naked and screaming and that all you have to do is stay away from it?"

"Now isn't that just perfectly brilliant."

Jacques had his head up but closed his eyes until the laughter of the class died down. And Guillaume slowly sat down having completely humiliated himself and pondered what he'd said and what had gone on and what had gone wrong. A demonstration was given on the application of purified alcohol to wounds as an antiseptic agent, something new in Andalusia having just been introduced in the early part of the century.

"Language does not merely report the world, rather language creates worlds, and in that creation is power. Tomorrow we begin the study of the pulse and urology, and that is all for today may Allah always be with you," said the professor.

"Come on, let's get out of here," announced Jacques.

"Yeah," Guillaume nodded, "but he never said I was right or wrong," and slowly got up and they went back to their apartment to put their books in and Jacques motioned Guillaume to come with him.

They wandered outside and Jacques kept motioning for Guillaume to follow him. In an hour of walking the young men came to a tavern, a Mozarabic tavern. They went in and sat down. A young man came over and asked them what they would have and Jacques said: "Two Frank beers, please."

The man went away and came back with two beers and laid them down on the table.

Guillaume said: "Music is my favorite way of thinking."

"Yeah, I know," stated Jacques. "And art is mine!"

Guillaume looked around and exclaimed: "Why is this place so quiet, what's the matter with everyone?"

"Oh, the Mozarabs are all down in the mouth right now and angry at the new regulations that the Caliph has imposed on them because of the wars. They think that their little place in Arabic paradise or Mozarab Heaven has now become Mozarabic Purgatory or perhaps Mozarabic Hell. And they no longer appear to be amused by Arabs."

The young men drank their beer very quietly. And then they stared out the window.

Suddenly a woman turned around on her bar stool, spoke up and said: "Kiss it, kiss it, you know you want to, you dooooo," she said spreading her legs very wide and hunching down in her chair.

No one said a word. It was deadly quiet. Then most of the people in the tavern suddenly broke out hysterically laughing and so did the brothers and they spilled their beer on each other.

They got up, paid their bill and left the tavern still chuckling heavily. Other laughing Mozarabs and a few amused Arabs also were leaving the tavern.

"Well, did that get your sensibilities up off the floor?" guffawed Jacques.

"Yeah, I guess so," laughed Guillaume.

"Don't let that teacher get you down, he's just a smart ass," Jacques said soothingly. "Can you believe what that woman said?"

And he laughed again.

"Let me tell you something, an Arab lover sent to his mistress a fan, a bunch of flowers, a silk tassel, some sugar-candy, and a piece of a cord of a musical instrument, and she replied by sending him back a piece of an aloe plant, three black cumin-seeds and a piece of a plant used in washing. His communication is thus interpreted. The fan, being called mirwahah, a word derived from a root which has among its meanings that of 'going to any place in the evening,' signified his wish to pay her an evening visit - the flowers that the interview would be in her garden - the tassel, being called shurrabeh, that they should have some wine, sharab, to drink - the sugar-candy, being termed sukkar nebat, and nebat also signifying 'we will pass the night,' denoted his desire to remain in her company until the morning - and the piece of cord, that they should be entertained by music. The interpretation of her answer is as follows. The piece of the aloe plant, which is called Sabbarah, it will live for many months without water, implied he must wait. The three black cumin-seeds explained to him that the period of delay should be three nights and the plant used in washing informed him that she should then have gone to the bath, and would meet him."

"That was quite charming and delightful. Are you that far ahead of me in Arabic?" asked Guillaume.

"Yes," said Jacques quietly, "about a year."

"And in medicine too?" he asked.

"Yes," replied Jacques.

"Well, I guess you're a better man than I," stated Guillaume.

"No, Guillaume, I'm not.   You see, intelligence is not the highest virtue, for it can be used for good or evil depending on the person.   Actually intelligence is not a virtue at all. It is the goodness of morality, either you are or you are not good or you will become good or evil. Satan smirks and he confuses us, and many of us are beset by illnesses or diseases, which make our temperaments unhealthy. You, Guillaume, are one of the good ones, potentially great ones, so it doesn't matter how highly or lowly intelligent you are.   Intelligence is more or less fixed. But morality is not. And you, my brother, are a better man than I. You see, I try, but you are and you grow. You have a great faith in the goodness of the world.   I see a huge war in this world between good and evil. One last thing: do you remember what Christ had to say? He said 'If you but had the faith of a mustard seed, you would move mountains', and it's true. Sorry, but I just couldn't resist that. It must be the pious preacher in me," said Jacques and laughed loudly.

Guillaume thought about that and all the other things all the way home.

"You mean if I have a wonderful attitude, and self-deceive myself about how wonderful the world is, then it will be so?"

At end of the year were the oral examinations, which both Guillaume and Jacques passed even higher than the year before. Guillaume was becoming a keenly observant man with a knack for pharmacology and Jacques for diagnosis in medicine. The two of them would put their heads together and learned medicine and pharmacology, thus deepening and widening their knowledge than each would have done alone. As a result they were given a modicum of respect from their fellows and teachers. They were beginning to make themselves fit in at last.

During that year, they learned a lot about surgery, and how to treat the body before and after. Their teachers brought in dead citizens to the school, to experiment and to learn on. The brothers did well, although Guillaume enjoyed it far more than Jacques.

The following year began again with oral examinations. And again Guillaume and Jacques passed, but not quite as high as the year before. They were both surpassed by three of the students in their class. These classes were the most rigorous of all, and the young men went to bed an hour earlier each evening. They were learning about compound medicines now, which would be the next to last resort surgery. The were also taught arithmetic which rankled Guillaume to no end until he found out that it was with a completely different kind of numbers.

At the end of the year, their third, they'd finished their medical training and were now able to practice under the watchful eyes of a physician. And for the next six months they began to learn through practice those theories they had learned in class. They made many mistakes and some almost constantly, but with the gentleness and direction of their physicians they began to come round, and gain a little more faith in themselves.

Two small clinics had been constructed: one in Cordoba, which administered to the poor, and the other in the palace, which administered to the wealthy. Each week the entire staff of one would replace the other, so that physicians would have a greater chance to practice their profession in Cordoba whereas they rested at the Palace where few came for medical attention being young, healthy and well nourished.

When their physician thought they were ready to take their oral examinations some of them took them early, and some later, eventually their whole class all took the orals and passed. They were being given a small education in medicine and expected to develop it to its fullest extent and go as far as they could depending upon our capacities. They were also told that their education did not come entirely free and that the Caliph expected some return on his expenditures: that each of them was expected to find new plants, to press them between pages to dry in order to have everyone know what kind of plant it was in the language of the country and in Arabic and all other languages and countries where the plant was found, as well as what beneficial medicinal qualities they might possess. Things had to be tested for results before mailing them here to the chief of physicians of the Great Cordoba Mosque if they found themselves in a different country other than Andalusia. In this manner Cordoba would get its money back for having spent it on our medical education.

Guillaume, tiring of constant classes, took a rest and walked for a time, again down by the Valley of the Mills. He could "see" the music of gentle breezes on the grasses waving and weaving, he could hear the tumultuous breezes rippling silently on his clothing. He did not know that other people could not see, hear, feel, and taste in the ways he could for he had never thought to ask anyone thinking it quite a normal experience. It was something that simply happened to him quite naturally. And after all, even his brothers could "see" the same things he did, so it did never occurred to either of them to ask anyone else. Eating the bread of Rosalinda had enhanced this way of "looking", and he felt that he had to sit down, and write her a letter via the Catalan translator at Santa Maria de Ripoll, thanking Rosalinda for the experience and also for showing them her successful new methods of administering medicine. There was much more to this woman than met the eye. She knew things about people without even asking them and was much more than an herbalist, he thought. It was getting late. He left that place and went home strolling and wondering and feeling a bit more affectionate towards Rosalinda.

The trees and bushes had their first beautiful dresses of greens and golds in the Spring and then faded into Summer with more robust changes of foliage and sober dark green dresses and new leaf growths rippling in the breezes with the expectation that summer would last forever. Guillaume and Jacques had more than satisfied their physician counselors that they were ready to practice medicine. And the day he stood up raising his right hand and took the oath of Hippocrates finally came at last. He and Jacques looked at one another hugged one another and laughed. They were newly minted doctors, but not yet physicians.

The government paid them a small stipend, enough to get out of their apartment and rent a home for the two of them in Cordoba on the street of the physicians. How joyous those days were for they couldn't help being happy. Their stipend would help keep them going until they could build up a practice. But reality was soon to break in upon them. For they were foreigners in a strange land who spoke a funny accentuated Arabic. And they had no reputation, and so most of the people who could come to them didn't and only the most poor did whom they rarely charged.

Month after month dragged by with little hope for improvement. Finally, Guillaume went into the bazaar and found an unemployed boy whom he hired to broadcast that there were now two new, and very excellent, doctors in town, in fact just up the street for whom they should go and see before the prices of these doctors went through the roof. The boy was ecstatic that he could now eat, and sleep in a home, instead of the streets, even had a job. Now he had a little money, which he could actually save. He thought he was rich! The small sum which Guillaume had "invested" paid off for there were now a tiny stream of paying people who came by and saw them, got to know them and found them to be just regular doctors like everyone else although they were Northerners whose Arabic was a bit peculiar.

And after their stipend ran out their stream of patients became a small river of ill people whose confidence in the doctors grew and their complaints became larger, more complicated and complex. There was a change in the attitudes and characteristics of the paying, working poor. They often asked for a talisman or charm, which they could hang around their necks. Guillaume and Jacques had already anticipated this and had gone out and gotten themselves amulets. At first it seemed to bother the brothers when people asked them for these trinkets, but then they saw the wisdom in it of advertising their "wares" to the populace. The young men began to learn how strong was the power of belief and decided that the patient's cure would go better with a positive attitude.

After some time they didn't really need the boy for advertising for them any longer and set him to keeping the house in good manner, going to the bazaar, cooking excellent meals for them and doing odd jobs for the brothers around the house. It had now been more than four years since they started their second round of medical studies and the year quickly changed into 960 A.D.

And then one morning it happened. A rider galloped up to the house threw himself off the horse banged on the door whose handle he soon tried and opened and in stepped the captain of the guards.

"Guillaume de Le Puy Valey?" shouted the man.

Guillaume was in the back, but came forward when he heard the ruckus.

"Yes," sounded Guillaume.

"Get your medical kit ready and come with me, quickly now, don't doddle," said the captain, "come on."

Guillaume gave Jacques a shrug and was out the door and up onto the back of the captain's horse. And they rode like hell was after them. Soon they were at the palace, jumped off the horse and ran into the Caliph's bedroom where the Caliph was struggling and strangulating on the floor. He had already brought up some foam and was in dire need of medical attention. Guillaume told the man to get more help, to hold down the Caliph to keep him from struggling so he wouldn't hurt himself, and be easier to work with.

He gave the Caliph several glasses of a mixture of the balsam of Matariyya and a number of his other herbs ground with his mortar and pestle and exclaimed loudly for anyone to hear: "Where are all his physicians?"

"They are either gone on assignments and diplomatic missions or dead, Guillaume, you are the only one," said the captain, "but others are on their way here."

The captain seemed anxiously.

"Is he going to be all right?" he asked gently.

"Bring a warm blanket to put over him and help him warm up," said Guillaume. "Who were his attackers?"

"Berbers, I think, there is one over here who is still alive and mumbling something in a Berber dialect I don't understand," said the captain.

Other men came running now.

"He may still die," Guillaume said. "But at least he is warm and much more comfortable now. I'll have to stay with him until the crisis is over. And this Berber is still alive, you say, well, we'll have to stop the bleeding."

Guillaume bandaged up the man's arm first before giving him a sedative and an opium mixture which he soaked into a sponge and held up to the man's nose to still his pain when he awoke. All the rest of the conspirators were dead on the floors. The Berber continued to bleed so Guillaume made a styptic from frankincense and aloe mixed with egg white to a consistency of honey and then adding a pinch of clippings from the fur of a hare. Unfortunately, the styptic did not work either. So, a hot fire was brought to Guillaume with an instrument to heat red-hot and he cauterized the wound then applying an ointment made of verdigris, wax and oil. Even under a large dose of opium the Berber whimpered.

Al-Zahrawi, the budding young surgeon came running in up to the scene and quietly looked it over. He asked Guillaume what he had given the Caliph, Guillaume told him about the oil and Al-Zahrawi nodded.

"You did well," said physician. "Now all we can do is wait. The greatest theriac is patience."

The Caliph vomited up some more of the substance, which Guillaume smelled but couldn't quite name. Still the theriac he gave to the Caliph was the correct one.

"You are to be congratulated, what is your name? Oh now, I recognize you," said al-Zahrawi.

"My name is Guillaume."

"I didn't think any Northerners would have the medical training you've obviously had. You must have graduated from the School of Medicine here in the Mosque of Cordoba," said al-Zahrawi, "and I see that you've also had a little surgery."

"Yes."

He told a few of the gawkers standing around to bring some more hot water.

"Well, I can see that you've got everything under control here and there is no need for me to butt into your business so I'll bid you goodbye, Guillaume," said the surgeon.

The Caliph's color slowly came back over the next few days and the Berber lived and was confined to the palace's prison. The royal physicians also returned including the Caliph's wazier, Hasdai Ibn Shaprut, a Jew who was head of his Jewish community in Andalusia, chief physician to the Caliph, chief diplomat, and who had many other titles and honors he'd earned in his service to his country. He had just heard the Caliph had been poisoned while on a diplomatic mission to the North, and he too wanted to help the Caliph and to find out who was responsible for it. As soon as he got back he went directly to the Caliph and saw Guillaume napping with his head down while sitting up in a chair someone had brought him. He looked at the Caliph. There was nothing he could do, for everything had already been taken care of by Guillaume. Hasdai would have to talk to this man about his compounded theriac, Mithridatum one day, particularly his secret ingredients. He also went to check on the Berber and saw that he was alive although laying on his bed, and not in a talking mood. Then he returned to the upper palace and found the Caliph resting. Hasdai summoned a few of his physicians to watch over him. Then Hasdai woke up Guillaume and told him he did very well that the Caliph was now in good hands and he could go home and get some rest. He also told him that someone in the government would contact him in a month or so.

The captain of the guards then spoke to Guillaume: "You will remember me?"

"Yes, I will, captain, yes I will."

Guillaume went back home on a horse someone gave him and slept for two days. When he awoke, Jacques wanted to know all about what had happened. But Guillaume was starving and not in a talkative mood. After the meal he promptly went back to sleep for an entire day.

In the weeks that followed the brothers and their medical practice seemed to grow as word of what happened began to spread throughout the palace. Guillaume marveled at the numbers of people outside his front door who wished to be treated. So they worked hard to accommodate them all.

The great festivals came, first the Feast of the Epiphany on Janurary 6th, and then people getting ready to travel to Mekka. Followed by the Great Festival, Eid Al-Adha. And then one day the captain of the guards rode up and called Guillaume to the front of his house. He told him that he was wanted at the palace tomorrow evening. The captain would escort Guillaume to the palace.

"Well," said Guillaume, "I don't know what to say."

The captain said, "I'll be here at twilight."

The next evening Guillaume and the captain rode up to the Rich Salon; that part of the palace on the highest part of the sculpted landscape in which the palace was cut in downward sections on a slope so that everyone could see the magnificence of the layout. Guillaume had never seen the palace at this time and thought how beautiful it all seemed, with the reflecting pools, where the fish broke the water making interlocking rings on it in the fading sunlight. There were fountains spreading water. He hesitated on the steps with the captain who had seen all this before and had other concerns to deal with. "Come on, Guillaume, they are waiting."

Inside there was laughter and young girls came and went bearing foods, sweetmeats and other delicacies. Men were discussing politics.

The captain led him on into the receiving chamber where the Caliph, Abd ar-Rahman III al-Nasr, stood on a slight platform and beneath it there was a large number of high officials. Hasdai came over to Guillaume and escorted him on in as if Guillaume was reluctant to receive his due.

He was given a heavy and beautiful ivory box, wrapped in a shawl of suf al-bahr, or sea-wool, which was a silk-like material, but with iridescence to it and worn only by the royal family. The ivory box with a truncated pyramidal lid of highly detailed carving of what looked like a sitting Christian holding a short scythe with two children; one on either side with a shepherd's staff and the other with a woven flag. All of this was inside a medallion with eight curved sides of interlocking knotted ropes. Exquisite hinges and locks of gold secured the lid. Around the lid were Arabic words in an early Kufic style, which at the moment Guillaume could not read. He opened the lid and nearly dropped the box for in the bottom and halfway up were gold Dinars and many pearls, diamonds, rubies, and a few emeralds. And some of the pearls fell out of the box and dropped onto the marble floor.

A number of men laughed under their breath and a few bent down to help pick up the pearls.

Guillaume said directly to the Caliph: "May you live in good health for a long time, and this is the second time you have honored me, my Lord."

The Caliph looked at him, slowly nodded, and turned away. People did not address him directly and there was a loud gasp in the chamber, but presently the Caliph turned and slowly walked away talking to his councilors.

The man next to him laughed and said: "I gather you've never been honored that much before?"

"It's the first time, I cannot believe how much wealth is in this box."

"The Caliph, my father, believes his life is valuable and has made a public demonstration of it, by giving someone like you, who has saved his life, the very essence of his wealth."

"He is your father?" said Guillaume.

"Yes," said Al-Hakam II, "I have been authorized to make you, should you wish, an assistant physician here in the palace and you have been made a noble of my family. So how does it feel to have been instantly made a distant relative of this family?"

"I don't know, perhaps I can grow into it," replied Guillaume.

His hand was being held affectionately by Al-Hakam.

"Come with us, tonight is your night and we'll dine until the late hours and you can tell us your life story or whatever story you can make up," said a comedian and a noble.

So, from that moment on Guillaume was a noble, a man of respect, a friend, a member of the family, and a knight of the Caliph's realm. And with great honor go great responsibilities. He told his hosts that he had been a noble once before as a child before the famines and how at age ten he had been given to the Church in Le Puy for his family couldn't afford the expense of feeding him and had studied herbs there but went south to Cordoba at the Caliph's generous bidding and had studied medicine in the Mosque.

Late that evening Al-Hakam who had been sitting next to Guillaume all evening leaned over and said: "I will pick you up tomorrow morning on my horse and we will go riding."

"That's fine because I can leave my brother with all the patients who've been coming around for weeks." Guillaume laughed.

On the way out, Guillaume took a large ruby out of his box in his concealed hand and put it surreptitiously into the open hand of the smiling Captain as he left with the audience as if he were merely and publicly shaking the man's hand.

The next morning Al-Hakam rode up to Guillaume's door at the palace, Guillaume came out, got up on the huge black horse behind Caliph's son and they rode back to the grounds near the palace. They stopped near a little ranch with a large corral in the back and a two-story house beside it. In the corral was a stunningly good-looking white horse, which was galloping round and round the corral. It turned out that Al-Hakam knew horses more than anyone. But he was in for a surprise for Guillaume also knew horses as his father used to sell them. They dismounted and leaned on the corral's fence and Al-Hakam began first to talk about the horse in front of him.

"His name is Sherrak, he is silent and soundless."

Al-Hakam looked at Guillaume quizzingly and said: "Do you see the muscles under his chest…"

"Looks like fehda, the female cheetah, doesn't she?" said Guillaume.

"The bird…"

"Yes, …Asfur, the top of the forehead and the prominences on each side of it, also a narrow star."

"And the Nahid…"

"The young sand grouse or muscle of the forearms," laughed Guillaume.

"And his Kamah…" said Al-Hakam.

"The expression of the eye like a vulture."

"For every noble horse that neighs…"

Guillaume finished it: "…a hundred asses set up their discords."

" I can't beat you, Christian, and this is the best I know of horses, he is yours, but where did you learn all this?" asked Al-Hakam.

"You are giving me this horse?" Guillaume croaked.

"And the ranch with which to keep him and of course you need a place to live, the house as well and two servants to look after it," said Al-Hakam. "All this has been given to you for the Caliph values his royal life highly for you have saved, perhaps saved Andalusia. We Arabs are noted for exaggerating ourselves. Still, you now understand our sentiment, and our extravagance."

Guillaume was dumbfounded. He began to realize that he was now a rich man beyond his wildest dreams.

"Would you like to ride him?"

"Yes. I think so," said Guillaume.

Al-Hakam II clapped his hands and one of the slaves of the house came out, saddled and bridled up the horse and walked the horse over to where Guillaume was and gave him the reins. He stroked the horse's face and long body with his hand and then the other side until the animal began knowing him and his tenderness. Then he got on easily and rode in a trot around the corral.

"Bravo, bravo, well done, you are a born rider, and you sit well, you must come with me to the polo matches, one day soon, and you shall have to show me how well you can ride," said Al-Hakam.

"My father put me on a horse when I was seven or eight and I rode constantly practically every day until my tenth year and still did so upon occasion when I was in the Church," explained Guillaume.

"Can you ride bareback as well like our cavalry," Al-Hakam said.

"Sure, why not?"

He took the saddle off and the soft white short blanket and swung up on the horse quite easily, grabbing the mane of the horse to help push himself up closer to the neck and he slapped the horse on his backsides. The horse and the man leapt into the air, kicking the air with its forelegs. It made a great impression on the Caliph's son.

"Lovely, lovely," he said. "Take it, take it all."

And so Guillaume met his slaves, an old man and his wrinkled wife. They were Arabs and they told him they took care of the place and he would not have any problems with the ranch.

Guillaume went home and informed Jacques about what had happened. He was as excited as Guillaume. He began making arrangements to live in the palace, where a place was already made for him with four rooms.

"Do you want to come and live on the ranch?" Guillaume asked Jacques.

"No, I'll stay here and work the practice."

Once Guillaume had made himself comfortable in his new quarters he began parceling out his fortune; first, to his family he gave a fourth, and to the bishop a fourth for the abbey to build a scriptorium and an infirmary, to Jacques another fourth, the last being for himself.

He searched through the corridors and found the man of the post and gave him instructions for insurance, and his letters to his parents, his older brother and the bishop.

In preparing for his new job, Guillaume found he had little to do other than to "be around."

After a few months he began to miss his old practice. With time on his hands he felt stale as though he were going nowhere. But that's the way it was for assistant physicians.

So he signed out, every physician had to do that so that someone there at Government House who needed a physician could see who was on duty and that there would always be someone on duty. And in the afternoons Guillaume went back to his residence to help Jacques out with his practice.

One day Hasdai stopped for a visit and he and Guillaume went for a walk. They came into a new section of the palace, still unfamiliar for Guillaume.

"This way, in here," Hasdai commented.

They went into a room, then into another and still another. Hasdai's secretary, Menahem ben Saruk came in and after talking to Hasdai left the room for a few minutes and then he came back in and sat down.

"I want you to look at something, Guillaume," said Hasdai.

On a low table was a stand and on it was a large closed book.

"Open it," said the chief court physician.

Guillaume sat down on the cushion and slowly opened the lock with hinges on it and turned over the cover.

"Ah-hah!" he said. "I've a feeling that this book was by Dioscorides, isn't it?"

"That's correct," Hasdai said. "Can you read Greek?"

"No, no, I can't," he said, "my brother knows much more than I."

"I am sure that you can read this one," Hasdai said, while putting another book on the table.

Meanwhile Ishaq Ibn Haytham and Abu Abdillah As-Sakili of Sicily came in and sat down. They were joined a few minutes later by Al-Busabisi and Abu 'Othman Al-Jezzar known as Al-Yabisah, all distinguished looking men whom Guillaume did not know. He nodded towards them in recognition and put this book on the upright stand next to the Greek text of Dioscorides. Ibn Al-Kattani and a Byzantine Greek monk named Nicolaus also came in and sat down. Next, in came a teenager whose name was Sulaiman Ibn Hassan Ibn Juljul and quietly sat down, followed by Ibn Samajun, another teenager. These books were the great works on plants, one with paintings of them, along with descriptions.

"Well, my Arabic writing is just so-so, but I could probably read it slowly, it seems the title is called Book of Herbs?"

"I believe they are the same book, but I very much like the illustrations in the Byzantine book." Guillaume said. "The first one is beyond me."

Abu 'Abd Allah Ibn Al-Qarani from Sicily came and sat down.

Hasdai said: "This is Stephan Ibn Basil's translation, which was revised by Hunayn. He was only interested in elaborating an Andalusi nomenclature, including Romance variations of plant names in order to adapt his text to our plants. You see, our dilemma is that the Byzantine Emperor sent this book as a gift to Abd Ar-Rahman III several years ago, but we couldn't understand it well enough to read it."

Mohammed Ibn Said, the physician came in and also sat down.

"Being in academic Greek, whereas the Greek I know is conversational of the streets. The Emperor sent us Nicolas a few years after our receiving the book, to help us. So, we are still in the same dilemma we were in before as we cannot translate and transliterate accurately the Greek of Dioscorides and yet our linguists are the best."

Mohammad, the botanist also joined the group.

Some directions from school were going through Guillaume's mind.

Hasdai said: "You see, this book was simply transcribed, but not really translated, parts of which were much less identified."

This fabulous team was expectant with any hope, perhaps this 'boy' could tell them something? Perhaps this group could push this on to a conclusion, to real findings, important findings?

"We will have to meet again, you and I and discuss these matters."

Guillaume thought about this and said: "My brother is an illustrator of bibles who can draw with ink and color good identifications of plants, realistically that is, just as they are. He has invented a strange new way of drawing. We have been going out into the fields and forests around here for some time looking for medicinal plants which we are struggling to give a name to, and which would be recognized by anyone looking at one in the field or in a book and we have them in alphabetical order in a kind of loose-leaf way so that one may study and place a plant out of place in order. We have already found some new uses for a few of your Andalusian medicinal plants."

Hasdai and a few of his colleagues looked up and at each other.

"Well," he said at least we are gaining strength, and perhaps some day we'll be able to decode the Herbal Book of Dioscorides very much like the decoding of Egyptian hieroglyphs by Ibn Wahshiyah in the last century, that's Abu Bakr Ahmad Ibn Wahshiyah, you see, he found that each glyph should be read phonetically and not seen as an object or an idea."

"Yes, I found his works in the archives one day when I wasn't looking for it, it's funny the way things like that happen, and there must be much else in private collections, I would imagine."

"He apparently used a piece of basalt with runes for words."

Then Hasdai began to introduce the gentlemen to Guillaume, all of whom could not come today, and Guillaume thanked him for what little he could do for them.

He left the meeting, deeply in thought and quite troubled about what more he could do to help these men. At the present time he could do no more than what he had already done.

When he saw Jacques he told him about the strange encounter with this group of men, and the books of Dioscorides and many other things connected with it.

Jacques said: "I'll think about it as we are going in that direction. I've had to let a number of patients go as I have been unable to see and work with them the way I'm used to and some I've referred to other physicians here in the neighborhood."

During his free time Guillaume began to study more elaborately Arabic calligraphy, but he never got good at it, as it had to be done with one's growing up with and in it. Perhaps Jacques could do much better?

He asked him if he thought he could make his calligraphy legible and Jacques thought that it was quite possible because calligraphy was an artistic activity, something he knew well.

ZARA

At the beginning of May the soil became dry and needed to be watered. The water, which had been in the reservoirs, was now released according to a pre-figured designed amount and the fields were watered. The water lasted until the rains came and began to refill the reservoirs. Snow melted on the mountains in May and came trickling down into the reservoirs as well and there was enough water to refresh all the fields. A very well paid man who had some social standing called the Leveler was responsible for designing all the irrigations systems as well as seeing to their being maintained.

Guillaume climbed up into the hills and mountains, watched the men coming and filling up the breaks in the soil with rocks. None of this was done in a mechanical manner or by rote, but by close observation. Water, for the Arabs, was everything. It was never wasted. The Leveler was also called the Water Master.

Guillaume descended the heights and facing the city stumbled down and down until he'd reached the bottom and walked back in a thoughtful manner all the way to the palace. He was invited by Hasdai to come to dinner. Guillaume brought Jacques with him for his brother had been working very hard for more than six months and at the same time gaining a good reputation as a doctor.

On the way over to Hasdai's home Guillaume remarked on what he'd discovered about the city's water supply and irrigation water from the mountains and wells in the area. And he talked a little about the different kinds of soil.

Jacques listened thoughtfully.

"Salaam aleikum," said Hasdai, "I am so glad you both could come tonight. We have a trio of young singing girls, who are unique in their field. We'll also have some talk about Dioscorides, which you might enjoy and fabulous food! But first the dinner!"

They went in and were immediately sprinkled with rosewater flavored sherbet and typical local sweets. Then they were handed glasses of drinks, which Guillaume didn't recognize and neither did Jacques. And they mingled with the guests.

All of the dinner was absolutely sumptuous.

"What a feast!" said Jacques.

"Yes," said Guillaume, "I agree."

While the servants the men wandered back into the sitting room with were clearing the dishes their drinks refreshed and congratulated Hasdai on the cooking.

And while they were resting they heard the song of Arab camel drivers--the Huda, from behind a curtain, a very old folk song.

Then one of the girls came out and began dancing with touching castanets while another hit the tambourine. Guillaume watched as the girl who was dancing took off scarf after scarf. Towards the end of the song she was nearly naked with just enough gossamer to partially clothe her body, as she slipped behind a curtain.

A second beautiful girl came out performing one of her own songs and did so on the spot. Her repertoire was said to be of some 4,000 songs, each with more than three or four verses. She was wearing a Jewish star in gold around her neck and began playing the lute beautifully, while the others played the bandore and the mizmar. There was high laughter all-around. Then this singer would change her mode, held her song for a few notes for a long time and the qithara or guitar and all other instruments played on.

The last delicious girl who came out was a shining-satined-black girl from Sudan who spoke perfect and melodious Arabic in reciting her poems. Sometimes one or two or all of them would be dancing with and without poetry. And after the performance they all thanked the gentlemen for having been quiet, attentive and had not tried to take advantage of them for singing and dancing was all they did.

"Some of their poetry is true wisdom," said Guillaume impressed by the girls.

"Yes," said Jacques thoughtfully, "it certainly was."

Then in came several young women not singers whom we were told were Muzna, A'isha, Safiya and Noiratedia, all who had a ready wit and delightful sallies had everyone laughing. A'isha was from Cordoba. One of the men who knew her said she was one of the most learned women of her age. Safiya was a learned poetess, and finally the slave Munza who acted as the Caliph's secretary and sang her own verses.

Then they all sat round the guests chatting with them for a while and making very pretty conversation as they wished to watch the second half of the performance.

Some more women came out with Radiya, a poetess and historian, who earned the admiration of all scholars in the East. And Maryam taught literature to the daughters of the leading families in Cordoba. And finally, Labna, well versed in many branches of knowledge, she was employed as Abd ar-Rahman III's confidential secretary who joined the other women. Then the girls all came out together with 'ud, tambourine and flute and commenced singing another lovely song.

Guillaume said: "That girl, I know her!"

"You do, you know her?" inquired Jacques.

"I mean I've seen her before."

"Where?"

"Oh, down by the Valley of the Mills, the Norias," Guillaume said.

"Oh, I see."

"You know, the one I told you about right after I saw her," said Guillaume.

"I remember now, the girl with the fur collar and cloak," he said, "She was wearing a red silken gown just like she's wearing tonight. I thought she was a Nabataean."

"So, her name is Zara, I think she is a Christian, and probably a Mozarab," at least that's what I think, perhaps born up North in Leon," said Guillaume,   "or maybe Castile."

There was still another performance: a pair of lovers having a passionate and very long song with one girl singing a boy's song. When the singing girls finished they all mingled with the crowd of middle-aged men. Guillaume slowly moved up to Zara and as he did so she caught sight of him out of the corner of her eye. She didn't move away. Yet she was somewhat curious and decided to wait and see what he might have to say. Guillaume stealthily glided up to her and nodded his head.   She continued to speak to the others but not to him. Guillaume was beginning to fall in love with this girl. He edged close to her and closer. Zara began to move away a little from him, suspiciously.   Finally, after an inordinate amount of time he had her alone.

"Yes?" she said, questioningly."

Guillaume cleared his throat and said: "That was a wonderful performance."

"I thought it was pretty bad, we're not in our best form tonight," said she.

"It was the first one I've ever seen."

"Oh, well, perhaps you will be able to see us again some other time?"

"I only want to see you," Guillaume said.

"Be careful, my friend," said Zarqun from Sudan: "She'll hang you and before she does she'll rip your heart out and stuff it down your throat, I know."

"Well, I'm sorry but you can't, as we only go about in threes for protection which of course here in Andalusia we really don't need," said Zara laughingly. "No, I eh, mean to see you for yourself."

"I'm not sure I know what you mean?" Zara said.

"I mean, eh, I eh, want to see you alone."

"Alone, you want to see me alone? Are you mad? Are you a fool, I'm a slave girl who just happens to have a wonderful master. You see, when I was ten I agreed to sell myself to my master who heard me singing one day, liked me and offered to buy me. My parents also agreed after I arranged to see them once a year and they were given a huge amount of money to live on far above their station. In no way would my parents have been able to rise to the station they are in now had I not done so. He also paid for my lessons, my singing, dancing, playing instruments and memorizing songs, excellent food and lodging. I owe him his investment besides what I owe him legally. I also owe him my life. I wouldn't change my status as a slave for anything. Imagine what would happen to me if I got caught up in seeing you. Hah! Who the hell are you, a monk who can't even marry inside his order?"

"No, I eh, I don't mean for that, I mean to, to, eh, speak together, is what I mean."

"Oh, certainly, what would you like to talk about?"

"Oh, anything will do."

"You're a strange one, what's your name?"

"Eh, my name, my name is ah, Guillaume de Le Puy en Valey."

"Well, my name is Zara," she said with finality.

"Where are you from, Zara?"

"I'm from up around Leon from a small town named Rueda."

"I'm from Languedoc."

"Oh, I see, a Northerner," said Zara smiling, "a stinking, barbarian."

"That is what many people think, but they are mistaken in their views."

"Well, you could fool me, but I knew those people around my town and they treated one another like barbarians, always arguing and ready for a fight, spying on their neighbors, would never do a lick of work for their community, or help the aged, those people's thoughts are in a pig stys and they lived in pig stys, they were very ignorant. Compared to them I live like a queen, my parents live like royalty."

"Oh, yes, I see now," said Guillaume.

"So, if you please, excuse me, I must get back to my companions."

"Oh, yes, I'm sorry."

As she moved off Guillaume felt as though something had finished in his life. There was simply a hole in his heart. He had unknowingly stumbled into a newfound love.

"Jacques, would you please come here?"

Jacques ended his conversation with one of the men, and half-grinning said: "Yes?"

"That woman actually told me I was a barbarian," Guillaume said indigently.

"Compared to them we probably are. Being a barbarian is a matter of geography with her, not only one's manners," said Jacques thoughtfully. "Look, it was just one of her little schemes being not likely to be loyal and true, besides what do you want with this slave girl? She can't ever be yours and you can never have her as long as you are Benedictine. She might not like you. So why worry about it?"

"Yes, you're probably correct," said Guillaume with a dumbfounded look on his face.

"This young woman who's been flirting with you has real talent for seductiveness and charm, in fact she ought to be congratulated on it. You see, she does her work well, my brother, particularly when she isn't performing, remember what the black girl said of your friend who would tear your heart out and shove it down your throat and then slowly hang you? She knows whereof she speaks. That girl sets traps you'll never get out of," Jacques said chuckling.

But Guillaume wasn't listening. His heart was already aching from her absence. He was a disturbed young man who'd just had his first encounter with the opposite sex and lost himself in the atmospherics of revelry.

"Oh, God!" Guillaume said.

Jacques looked at him, shook his head from side to side.

"Please, Guillaume, don't embarrass me here this evening, come on, change the look on your face, or I'll have to get a ride home and for God's sake, don't moan."

Al-Hakam II who had been at the back of the room came over and said: "Well, Guillaume how have you been?"

"Fairly well!

"I wonder, would you like to visit my father's library tomorrow?"

"Oh, yes, I would, I certainly would," said Guillaume excitedly.

"Good! Then I'll come by for you around nine in the morning," said Al-Hakam.

"That would be fine and thank you very much," replied Guillaume.

The scent of jasmine and gardenias nearly overpowered the men as they left Hasdai's party.

Guillaume took Jacques to his old home. Jacques had some prints he wanted to show Guillaume. They went in and in the lamplight Guillaume was astonished at the progress his brother had made in the months he had been away.

"They look pretty good, eh?" said Jacques.

"Yeah, they certainly do, said Guillaume, "these plants look so much better than the ones I've seen in the Dioscoride's Herbal Book that I am staggered. They look so life-like."

"You like them then?" asked Jacques.

"Oh, I sure do, can you do some more?"

"Yes, I will.

Jacques was grinning.

In the following days Guillaume had occasion to meet Zara again. In the halls of government house they passed one another. As Guillaume looked back at her she recognized him. Having heard of his being given a robe of honor brought to the surface in her a level of respect and perhaps some desire of power over him.

She laid her traps and spread her nets well. She ogled him, smiled too readily at him, even flirted with him, but he was not deceived by her antics. Now he was a bit standoffish and spoke to her not as a lovesick boy but as a man to another woman. He said his good-byes respectfully and walked away. She was nearly devastated for almost five minutes. Then she began cooking up other schemes to trap him.

That evening Guillaume went back to his palatial rooms and found there two letters for him from his bishop and his father. Opening the first, he began reading.

He first read the one from the bishop, who thanked him for sending them wealth and telling him that the monastery had been expanded. Thanks to the wealth from Guillaume, the monastery now could fully care for its sick.

The father's letter was a bit more sad, reminding Guillaume that he hadn't been in touch for two years. Of course, this made Guillaume feel very guilty. Nevertheless, the father had also told him that they had received the wealth he had sent.

Guillaume was depressed and didn't quite know what to do. He moped around the following days.

One evening he went to the river and sat down on the slightly rising slope next to a narrow stream. He lifted his wineskin to drink again letting out a thin but solid stream of wine about two feet long flow into his mouth. He'd already had too much. Looking at the Guadalquivir river's water slowly pass he thought he had seen it all before. The water mills were groaning again. But then they nearly always groaned until the high point of summer when the river began drying up. He looked up at the mills across the old Roman bridge into the darkness. Just then, a small wine glass came floating by on the narrow stream and surprised him. He picked it up and looked around in the dark.

A female voice said: "Won't you fill mine too?"

"Why not?" he said, placing the glass on the ground, then unplugging the wineskin and gently pouring some wine into the glass. He stuck his arm out in invitation to drink and the woman came over and sat down beside him.

"Thank you, Guillaume," she said and looked at him.

Guillaume was surprised and looked at her closely.

"Zara?"

"I know you think me cheap and the kind of woman who is low. One who cannot be fresh and you are right. One who has had many experiences with men and yet I am still a virgin. I promised myself when I was fourteen that I would save my heart for a loving man whom I would marry," Zara said.

"Yeah, I heard that all before, you see, I've been told about you, about singing girls, by you, and others, how you ogle us and how you run us down into the ground, you people are about as sincere as I am sober."

She began to cry softly leaning over towards the ground in a full-length position.

"You're not fooling me one bit," Guillaume said drunkenly.

Turning over she said, "I will be true to you, Guillaume, if you want me to."

Guillaume turned towards her weaving a little, tried to put his hand out to push her away slipped and his hand fell on her breast.

"Oh, I'm sorry, Zara," he said.

"That's all right," she said.

"You women are all the same. Not a true feeling in you. You put on an act as if you were on stage exciting the men for a little power and a lot of money," Guillaume said.

She pulled him down to her and kissed him on the mouth. He was too drunk to struggle much and then he didn't really want to. She took the rose in her hair and put it behind his ear. Their hearts were pounding and they were scared and frightened like rabbits. As there was no one about she took off her upper garment and pulled him down to her breasts.

The night darkened and over them wafted a bouquet of scents of orange blossoms, gardenias and jasmine. The sounds of groaning from the water mills in the river filled the air sounding like camels giving birth. And now and then a fish disturbed the waters, and fireflies were illuminating the evening with their tiny yellow lights. The night settled down into a deep cool slumber.

At dawn young boys brought their kites to display in the sky. All were made of Chinese paper, and all had music produced by a bow fastened to the neck which, once in the air, resonates in the wind making a melodious, droning sound. The pitch of the sound and the volume were rising with the speed of the wind. A boy who was experienced could tell whose kite it was by the 'song' of the kite.

There were now three boys who were joined by a fourth and then a fifth who was racing up the slope and into the wind, which launched his kite soaring into the air. Some kites were shaped like giant birds, some were boxes, and all were made of rattan or bamboo which could be had by the boys from traders and merchants off Mediterranean ships of long-distance ocean voyaging ships, and brought up from Seville to Cordoba. The merchants much enjoyed giving the boys something they could use, because the children were so grateful. Many kites were decorated and a few were huge. The largest kite was flown by a well-respected kite-master. He came that morning to display his kite in the sky. When it leaped into the air the old man was young once again.

At daylight Guillaume felt rather embarrassed, and fumbling with his clothes in order to straighten them out as he moved off the slope taking a long look at the kites flying in the sky before walking back to his home. He walked in seeing Jacques with one of his patients, waved to him that he was going back to the palace and Jacques nodded.

A week later Guillaume left for Seville on Gift with his now free ranch manager Juan happily riding next to him on a mare. A couple of pack donkeys ran in back of the horses.

And three months later when Zara didn't have her curses, she felt dizzy. And by the time she had her morning sickness she knew she was definitely pregnant. Her breasts had become harder and fuller and her stomach began to swell. She stopped singing and performing and out of her money she had saved up, paid her master off, 80.000 dinars. She was free. He had been very reluctant to let her purchase her freedom for she was making him a good deal of money, but he respected her wishes and she had paid off all the money he had invested in her and much more besides. This was pure profit. She could have given him five more years, after that she wouldn't be as excellent as she had been, but...

"Beauty is a fragile thing and doesn't linger," he said to himself.

Now he would have to find himself another to take her place. And that wouldn't be easy for she was among the very best.

Six months later Jacques stopped taking patients. He went up into the mountains overlooking Cordoba to pray and work with his friends, mystical Muslims.

APART

Guillaume and his man Juan arrived into Seville riding all along the Guadalquivir from Cordoba. The closer they got to Seville the more pleasure boats they saw. And the tree lined branches on either side of the banks crossed one another casting shadows on the river complemented the scene. They went down to the wharf with many ships and boats bobbing up and down in the windy sunlight. Guillaume stopped at the quay on the left side of the wharf and began asking captains if they needed another passenger for Montpellier. A number of them were going to Nice or Toulon or to Marseille but none for Montpellier. A few others said they would take him near Nimes, but he would have to pay more money, as it wouldn't be easy.

After a while he began to thrash his mind for having been so impetuous at not having sent down word he wanted to leave and to wait for a ship going in his direction. Finally, in the last half-dozen or so ships he found a captain who would take him along with a number of other passengers to Montpellier.

The bright sunlight reflecting off the seawater momentarily blinded him.

An Arab came up behind him and said: "Going south sir, I've got a pair of yellow cork sandals you might wish to give to your sweetheart?"

Closing his eyes and turning his head Guillaume looked again and again. He was blinded by bright work reflecting off the ships.

"Yeah, and I'll take 'em," said Guillaume.

The captain was friendly and helped him to place his four overly large leather saddlebags on this ship.

"I'll be going to Le Puy," Guillaume added for the sake of talk.

"I'll get you to Montpellier. No further than that," the captain said smiling.

Guillaume asked the man how much the fare was and pulled out his leather money pouch and paid him a number of dinars.

"We're not going for a couple of hours yet as we still have some loading to do, but there is a shop up the street which serves hot meals, I'm telling you this because I know the owner of the shop and I dine there. It's a reputable place," the captain commented.

Guillaume and Juan having relieved themselves of the baggage went on up the cobblestone street to find the shop the captain mentioned, they went in and were well seated for some delicious food.

"You won't have a problem getting half-way back before dark, and you will feed them all well?" asked Guillaume.

"No, it's no trouble at all, not for me. I will feed them well and in case you are delayed for some time I'll put Gift up for stud," laughed Juan.

"Oh, I should be back within a few months, but if not, give Gift to my brother Jacques, he lives in the last house on Physician's street," said Guillaume.

"I will do that," his man said.

"But I don't see any problem in my coming back by land as I want to see someone in Saint Marie de Ripoll," Guillaume intimated.

Then came their food, a Sevillian paella similar to the one from Valencia but with shrimp not chicken and a special white wine.

"Paella waits for no man, let's dine!" said Guillaume.

After discussing many things, Guillaume shook Juan's hands. He told Jaun what a good man he was. Guillaume paid for the dinner and gave some money to him for expenses on the way back. But the man wouldn't take it.

"You'll need it more than me," said Juan.

They left the dining establishment and Guillaume waved goodbye to him, Juan nodded and rode off with Gift in tow and the donkeys behind the horses. Slowly Guillaume walked back to the ship, the captain saw him and waved to him that they were leaving right away.

"May God's peace and blessings be upon you!"

It would be a very long time before Guillaume saw the tuberoses of Seville again.

The ship's lantern or mostly triangular sails filled out with the wind and like a full bosom pushed the ship out into the river all day through the swamps and down toward the sea.

The next day they rounded the Strait of Jabel Al-Tariq or Tariq's Mountain, sailing east.

The third day caught them in open sea with the waters swirling up, and down, and around them. The wind blew so mightily the captain had a few men trim the sails. They made good progress.

As Guillaume looked back he could barely see Barcelona and the white-tipped Pyrenees Mountains. Sea spray hit him in the face. But he didn't mind, and he began to enjoy his experience of long distance sailing. He looked around, and saw a dark speck on the horizon but thought nothing of it.

The captain said: "Abad, can you see it?"

Abad replied: "Can't make it out quite yet."

He could see far better and farther than most men his age or younger.

"I see him now, and I think we ought to hurry," said Abad quickly.

The captain called for more sail even though the winds were still a bit too strong for them. The speck became larger, and was moving in their direction. The captain made some nervous gestures, which Guillaume didn't understand. The crewmen were scrambling about trying to make the ship sail faster and faster. The speck became a ship, which was coming closer and closer to them all the time. Now some of the passengers were becoming nervous.

"Get out the weapons," yelled the captain calmly, trying not to act nervous.

The ship was now so large to be recognized as a Sicilian pirate ship coming straight at them. The captain told the passengers to get below in the hold, and they complied very nervously and quickly, not wanting to be part of any trouble. Some of the men had come up from below with many bows and arrows, throwing lances, and knives, which they quickly passed out. There were a few crossbows as well.

The ship came so close that the pirates could throw lances and hit one of the men. A crossbowman made quick work of the pirate. More lances were thrown most missing the men. Guillaume peeked out from below decks, but quickly brought his head back inside as the lances were coming thicker and faster now and posed a clear danger to him.

There was a huge bump, and crash as the pirate ship with its metal-headed battering ram smashed into the merchant ship. Cries were heard as those below saw seawater rushing in the hold of the ship.

There was another speck on the horizon, but no one saw it.

Fighting broke out on all sides as men plunged into the thick of war. Guillaume came out of the hold, found a lance on the ship's hull and threw it back at one of the pirates. The spear caught the man in his neck and he quickly folded over. Another pirate came at him with a sword, and swung, but Guillaume ducked, and hit the man with his large fist bowling him over. Just as he straightened up another arrow lance was coming at him, and he ducked that one too.

At that moment an arrow shot from a pirate's crossbow on board the pirate ship hit Guillaume in his upper left shoulder knocking him backwards completely off the ship. A raft of broken boards half-threaded together lay directly in Guillaume's path on which he hit with enough force to knock him out. His raft slowly drifted away from the now burning ship.

The fighting was still going on, but the speck had now become large enough to make it out. It was a ship of the Caliph's naval patrol ships on duty in that area sailing quickly forward to take on the pirate ship. It came on and on and finally was beside the pirate ship.

Guillaume's raft floated further away from the fighting, and the men were all completely exhausted, some were wounded, some lightly, some badly and needed attending. The bodies of the pirate ship were unceremoniously thrown overboard and the passengers were escorted onto the navy ship. The dead captain of the merchant ship was brought over just in time for the burning, and the half-crushed ship as it collapsed into pieces in the sea.

The raft on which Guillaume lay had barely enough buoyancy to keep him afloat. The lower part of his leg slipped over the ship's boards, and washed in the sea. His leather sandal slipped off his foot. Slowly spinning round and round the sandal went down into the depths of the indigo sea.

The waves began to rise and fall and slap against the raft with Guillaume throwing his arm over on his chest, and back again. Restless he stirred once putting his arm on the arrow stuck deep into his left shoulder, and then slowly drifted off into a deep coma.

The sky darkened, and the waves became choppier. Tiny fish swam up to the falling sandal giving it a quick bite. Then the sea became quieter for a moment.

Something in the depths began to move and moving made the seawater shift faster and faster. It broke on the surface in a huge spray hitting the raft with sea spray. For two days and nights Guillaume floated and drifted along in the Mediterranean. The dawning sun came up and out from behind the clouds. Near the horizon a ship sailing along didn't notice Guillaume until it got very close.

"Man in the sea, man in the sea," said someone and pointed at him.

The captain ordered the men of his ship to trim its sails, and told a few of them to get into a small skiff and row out to the man.

Grabbing him as gently as they could, he cried out once and they put him in the small boat and rowed back to the ship. Someone got a long wide piece of lumber shaped like a door and gave it to the men in the skiff. They slid the wood under him, and let down a couple of ropes from above on a wooden crane, and then attached one rope to the end of the wood and the other to the other side. This way they hauled him aboard.

The captain looked at him and said: "Well, I don't see any black flesh, nothing rotting, must have been the salt in the seawater preventing him from becoming infected.   But once we get that arrow out we'll have to cauterize him.   Stoke up the fire ironman!"

Lifting him up the Arab captain touched Guillaume's back where the arrow should have come out to see if it had gone completely through his shoulder.

"Yes, I can feel the point," said the captain and for a few minutes continued to examine Guillaume.

The point barely pointed up to the skin and Guillaume groaned. The captain nodded.

"Are the irons ready, yet?"

"Just about, captain, just about," said the ironman.

"All right, hold him tight and keep your body to the right so when I shove the arrow through his shoulder you won't get hurt when the arrow goes through."

"Yes."

The captain shoved the arrow with all his might in Guillaume's shoulder and it pierced the skin of his upper back. Guillaume let out a scream and groaned. The captain took a cloth he had with him and put it on the arrow's tip and pulled the arrow on, all the way through.   Blood splattered everywhere.

"Ironman quick!" said the captain.

The captain took the iron and plunged it into the wound in Guillaume's front shoulder and took another iron to cauterize him in the back. Guillaume screamed and continued moaning, but never awoke from his coma.

"Alright. Now lay him down gently," growled the captain.   "And fetch me a couple of dry blankets."

In rolling Guillaume over to place the blanket beneath him, and taking off his clothes they felt something metallic inside a square piece of cloth sewed to his outer garment which hit the wood of the ship with a clanking sound. Opening the flap the captain reached inside and found a star finder.

"Aha," said captain Abdullah, "what's this?"

He pulled it out and began to look at it, turned it over and saw that it was a latitude independent astrolabe or better known as a universal astrolabe, which one could use for all latitudes above the equator. Each line inward was scrolled in a circle, a smaller circle than the last, and instead of these circular lines meeting in a circle in the middle they were scrolled circles at the top, and bottom of the heavy brass object as they would normally be at the poles. He read the name inscribed at the top: Ibn Az-Zarqallu of Toledo, 328 A.H. He turned it over to look at the back.

"So this is al-Safihat, the plate of climate by Al-Zarqallu, I've been hearing about," said the captain. "But you can't use this on a rolling ship or in the wind or when it has clouded over," he said to no one in particular and his thoughts began drifting back to when he was a young man in school.

The captain put all the pieces back into the Guillaume's folded square.

"It's too bad his star charts are all wet, now this thing is useless."

"Come on, let's get this man to my cabin now we need not simply want to save his life for he's a nobleman."

Several men picked up Guillaume and with some difficulty brought him into the captain's cabin.

Captain Abdullah spotted something else around Guillaume's waist picked it up took out his knife and sliced the leather string, which carried the bag. Quickly putting the bag in his pocket the captain took the other blanket, and covered Guillaume rubbing him lightly. He groaned.

"Get my medical kit down and bring it over here," said the captain.

His kit was brought and the captain took out a small jar of opium and with his finger, rubbed some of the opium out on it, and put some on Guillaume's lips, and then in his mouth and tongue. He took some white cloth and ripped it into squares for a bandage, putting one on top and another on the backside of the man. Then he took a roll of the same bandages and telling one of his men to hold him up strapped it around his shoulder and in the back. Then he placed his hand on the man's forehead and felt his temperature. Before leaving he looked at Guillaume one last time and went out of his cabin.

The captain gazed around the horizon and seeing nothing, directed the men to the take out the sails again and let the wind take his ship.

"Alright, he'll sleep the opium off for a few days."

The weather began to clear up. The sun came out and everything slowly started drying out. The men took off their oilskins, and got into dry summer clothing.

Guillaume stirred but went back to sleep. The Captain knew that Guillaume was a noble for only a noble would have carried that much wealth with him in such a small bag tied around his waist. He looked at the jewels turning them over in his hand then he hid them in his locked iron trunk.

Several days later Guillaume woke up and then realized his shoulder hurt him terribly and he groaned again. This time he was awake.

The captain Abdullah walked over to him and looked at him.

"Well, awakened from the dead, huh?"

Guillaume asked in Latin: "Oh, where am I?"

"You're on my ship, and we're heading for Alexandria," said the Arab captain who knew Latin.

Guillaume fainted, again.

"It looks like he'll live, and might bring in a great ransom," said the captain smiling at the thought.

It was three weeks before Guillaume could sit up for a few minutes drink his water, and eat a little rice. He reached down and felt the string, but the pouch had been lost.

In another week the captain docked his ship in Alexandria. Guillaume finally got up, but he was extremely weak and shaky. The next day he managed by himself, threw off his blankets and nearly fell over, but stood and put on his ragged clothes. Several days later the captain came in and asked Guillaume if he wanted to buy some new clothes. Guillaume nodded.

"Come on then," said the captain as they waited until someone boarded the boat ladder with a heavy load.

They walked up the street a bit and found a clothing shop. Going in captain Abdullah saluted the proprietor and asked him to show them some clothing for a nobleman. The clothier had a number of items for sale, and Guillaume picked out a rather nice one. The captain paid the man. All of which disturbed Guillaume as he had wanted to pay, but his money belt had vanished in the storm, and now his pouch too was missing.

The captain looked at him, and looked at him up and down and then bought a soft square leather bag for Guillaume's astrolabe. He quickly put it in and handed it to Guillaume.

"Take those rags and burn them, no, wait a minute, I'll keep them for you. You may need them again."

The proprietor nodded and showed them the way out.

"Now we'll get ourselves a nice bath."

They walked up the street further until they found a bathhouse. When they came out after some hours they looked and felt like new men.

Then they got something to eat. Guillaume's shoulder still hurt him badly, and he was walking with almost a lean. The captain noticed this.

"There is a ship leaving in a week or two. My cousin, Solomon, is the pilot. He always leaves about this time of the season. Even the Caliph gets in on the trade, and Solomon works for him and has the largest ship I've ever seen," said the captain.

He tossed Guillaume the pouch with his jewels in it.

"And, I'll be taking this one," he held up a small emerald which glinted in the sunlight.

Seeing the look of surprise on Guillaume's face the captain continued.

"This is for saving your life, helping you with your wound, and transporting you to Alexandra," said captain Abdullah again smiling.

"Oh, God, it's easily yours for all your trouble," replied Guillaume laughing.

"Now listen, I'm going to give you some excellent advice for I heard you raving on and on about having to do this and that, and going back to Andalusia when all you wanted to do was find new drugs possibly in distant lands. My cousin has a great ship and needs a ship's doctor, I know this because I just got a letter from him a couple of days ago. He is going to India in about a month's time and I believe you should go with him. A young man like you with no wife on his hands, no commitments, not settled down yet, it's made for you as a professional man.

"Where is his ship leaving from?" asked Guillaume.

"It is docked at the upper end of Bahr Al-Ahmar, the Red Sea, and you could get to

Fustat from here in Alexandria, and from Fustat you would have to travel by camel caravan to the Red Sea," said captain Abdullah and smiled.

"I don't know," Guillaume was puzzled," I don't know."

"Oh, come on, it would only be for a few months," said the captain.

"Well, maybe you're right, but I don't know how to get to a camel caravan or how to ride or anything," countered Guillaume in a complaining tone.

"Come on, I'll show you how," laughed the captain.

They walked on until they came to the caravans where all the camels were kept on the outskirts of town.

Then the captain shouted out: "My friend seeks to go to Fustat by camel. Who will give me the lowest price?"

Three or four men rapidly came up, and began quoting prices, the captain picked one of the men and asked: "Can you take him to the Red Sea?"

"Yes, I'll take him," said the exasperated camel driver.

"And when can you do that?" asked the captain.

"Why, now, I am ready to go, simply waiting for the sun to go down, but with an extra man, I can go now or a little later," said the man.

"Good," said the captain. "Well, there you go, do you know how to handle these people, these ships of the desert now, these Bedu? You have to stand up for yourself."

"Yes," said Guillaume.

"And here are some traveling clothes for you to wear, your rags, for if you are caught wearing those wealthy man's clothes you'll be robbed for sure."

"How did you know I was going to go since you had already bought those clothes?" asked Guillaume.

The captain laughed.

"It was written all over your face."

Guillaume thanked him for all he had done and shook his hand.

The captain returned his salute in Arabic style to Guillaume.

"May Allah watch over you, and the One who is Master of us all, young man."

Guillaume watched for a long time as captain Abdullah disappeared and then he turned to the camel driver.

"When exactly are you going?" he asked.

"Oh, well, maybe not for a few hours yet," said the indecisive camel driver.

"Then I must go into town to get some money, and write a quick letter," said Guillaume.

"Sure, go ahead, but be back before I go," said the camel.

Guillaume shook his head at the Arab's words. His shoulder ached him, but he began to hurry his steps towards town and he stopped at the jewelers and got a good price. So he sold a few of his precious jewels.

Then he went next to the market and bought an empty medical kit, which he could use at sea. The new supplies he bought from a traditional pharmacist's stand. Then he went to the letter writer's bench, and asked a scribe to write down his message to Jacques, and gave the man the money he requested.

The man said, "I'll send it on from the postal system here to Andalusia."

Guillaume turned and walked back to the outskirts of town where the camel caravans were, just in time to get a camel for himself and then slowly they were off on their journey.

The sky was beginning to change. He looked around from his vantage point, and felt strange with the back, and forth movement and it took all the rest of the day to feel comfortable. He very much missed his horse, Gift.

"You need to get out of those clothes, young man," said an older man who looked well off yet was wearing some of the meanest clothes he'd ever seen.

"Why is that?" asked Guillaume.

"Because if we are stopped by bandits, you will be the first, and most roughly taken to task perhaps, or captured for ransom, even killed," said the stranger, "they all know already where we are headed, to Fustat and are involved with that town's police for half the good's the bandits get from us,"

Guillaume reached in his bag for the ragged clothes and changed.

The camels were going steadily and after several days the sand began to come down like rain, and pelted them. Swirling this way and that, they were getting sand in their mouths and placed part of the turban windings around the lower part of their faces. Sand got in everywhere, and in everything. For many days they continued their way, the camels knew the route.

And then it suddenly became black in the middle of the day and the camel driver stopped the caravan, the sand storm was too intense. For two days, Guillaume slept with his turban cloth over his head.

When sand storm ceased he and the rest of his caravan saw a line of mean looking men on camels with their lances, daggers and swords readied for war, looking at them menacingly like hungry vultures.

Two of them got down from their camels and began to go through everyone's baggage. Since they didn't find anything worth stealing they started hitting and pounding the old camel driver who cried out. This made the people of the caravan very uneasy.

Seeing this Guillaume and another man abruptly startled the bandits by jumping on the two men, while the rest of the caravan having got the idea also began screaming wildly at the bandits most of whom were still on their camels.

Guillaume pushed the struggling man's head into the sand and held it there while the man flailed about his arms and legs hitting Guillaume in his attempts to breathe. After a few minutes the man's struggling lessened, but Guillaume held the man's head hard against the sand. His companion had slit the other bandit's throat, wiped his dagger on the man's clothing and started running after the other bandits. This so startled the robbers that they all galloped away.

Finally the man on the ground stopped breathing and Guillaume brought his hands up and looked at them for this was the first time he had ever killed a man. His heart raced and pounded, his chest was shaking and his legs wobbly, yet he got up and went to the camel driver to see how he was. The man was badly bruised but alive. Guillaume gave the man something to drink and the man thanked him.

After a while everybody was ready to go, they mounted their camels, even the camel driver. The wind had died down by now. And then the caravan continued.

Ten days later they came into Fustat and the city's police looked at them surly, but without taking them to task. The caravan stopped for the day in Fustat to get fresh water and supplies.

The next day early, they went back into the desert, heading toward Suweis and the Red Sea, where the ships were waiting for them.

Several days later they came into Suweis and saw the ships stacked row on row along the wharves. Guillaume paid the camel driver and gave him some ointment to put on his body. Then Guillaume took his medical kit and clothes and began searching the ships for the SeaWolf. After some time he found it, it was the largest ship there with nearly 200 feet long. Guillaume asked a man if they needed a doctor?

"We do! Are you a doctor?"

Guillaume replied: "Yes, I am."

"Well, come aboard, then," said the man.

Guillaume began walking to the gangplank and up the steps and into the huge ship.

"Where are you going? And your name is?" quizzed the man.

"Guillaume de Le Puy en Valey."

"Ah," said the man, "so you're the person my cousin told me about in his letter."

"And you are?" Guillaume asked.

"The pilot, my name is Solomon."

He was a fat man and bald-headed.

"And where will you be sailing to?" Guillaume asked.

"To the far ends of the earth," laughed Solomon as he looked down on the decking of the ship.

At that moment something passed in front of the sun and cast a shadow on the deck, Solomon with a gold earring hanging from his earlobe looked up to see a sea gull. Guillaume looked at Solomon's neck and could easily see a rim of muscle surrounding the upper portion of the man's neck.

"Let me see your astrolabe, young man," said Solomon.

"How did you know I have one?" asked Guillaume.

"Because of your pocket sagging and the medium-sized square pocket stitched into your clothing, and because my cousin wrote about it in his letter," said the pilot.

Very little passed by this man's observational sense without being noticed. Guillaume took it out and let Solomon see his astrolabe.

"Yeah," the pilot remarked, "I've seen these before. The astrolabe is a toy. Something invented and improved on by mathematicians of the Greeks and further developed by the Arabs. And what do scholars know? The only thing they know is in books. They have no experience. Certainly the scholars have no experience in leading men to organize a ship and make it go in the direction you want."

He spat into the waves.

"They are also very slow, for by the time one asks one of them a question and the time you get an answer, a ship could be lost through a scholar's indecision or delay," said Solomon, "all right men, raise the second sail, it's time we got under way."

The pilot spoke with such a commanding voice that the men quickly obeyed him.

Solomon's pilgrims were getting restless. A large group of them were on board together to be dropped off at the port of

Jeddah and would then continue to travel by land to Mekka and Medina.

The ship with her smaller mizzen sail unfurled began to move out from her slip into the sea and everyone took a deep breath from the coolness of the breeze. The sky was cloudless.

Out on the sea the lateen sail was unfurled. The main mast was about 100 feet above the deck. The pilgrim's began to relax.

Solomon continued his verbal cannonade.

"Scholars," he said as if the word were a dirty, filthy one. "Scholars, they couldn't find their private parts in broad daylight let alone the latitude."

He looked surreptitiously at Guillaume out of the corner of his eye.

"Scholars are the most stodgy pedants and students of ambiguity such as the world has ever seen, hah! Do they even know where to buy and sell timber, and at what time, and other goods, to find the best teak for example for building ships or making fine furniture? Do they know the price of goods in one place and how much to sell it in another? All Scholars know is how to stand up before an audience and pontificate utter nonsense about one thing or another and write books. Or they argue amongst one another, endlessly debating some fictional point and forgetting to put one's hand in the water to find out for themselves, whether the water is hot or cold! Hah!" said the pilot. "Every argument must be grounded in the concreteness of experience."

Solomon looked over at Guillaume and seeing the wrinkles on his face and he chuckled under his breath.

"Do they know how to steer by the stars without an astrolabe or kamal, I don't think so," said Solomon, "a scholar would merely be in the way out here. You will need sea clothes, you can't wear what you've got on," Solomon gestured to him. "Your cabin is on the left side of the ship, there," he said.

Guillaume walked to his cabin and went inside. He pulled his brass astrolabe out of his clothing and laid it on the bed. Then he took off the strap, which held his medical kit on his shoulder and put the kit on the tiny desk. And at last he threw his bundle of clothing on the bed. There was a knock at the door, someone opened it and gave him his simple sailor's clothes for daily wearing and a second pair for changing in rough weather.

Solomon had his first mate take over steering the ship. He then went to his cabin and looked at his well-used astrolabe hung up on the wall. Then he searched for a chart of the Red Sea, it was among his many books. Unfolding it he placed it on his desk and found the port of Jeddah. All his talk to Guillaume about scholars was just that: talk. For the pilot was much more than a navigator, besides being a scholar of the sea he was also a first class merchant. He had wanted to take the measure of Guillaume to know how long and how deep his mind was, knowing he would be impressed by scholars and having done so would now try to teach him a little navigation, as his first mate would never amount to anything beyond what he was told. He couldn't take initiative and would sink the ship.

Solomon took the kamal off a hook on the wall and decided to teach him what he could. He figured it would take him fifteen or 16 days sailing at eight knots an hour to reach At-Turbah, if all went well, and another day to reach Aden, their first trading post. This might become a journey of perhaps a year or two at most. He looked at Jeddah again, which he had seen many times before on the map, and then folded it up and put it away.

In a few days time they sailed down to the port of Jeddah near Mekka, letting off the pilgrims. They cleaned the ship of all the debris with seawater and then gave themselves a little rest. Then they sailed on down the Red Sea and around the point at At-Turbah and into the Gulf of Aden and the sea of Berbera. As they had nothing to buy or sell at the great market city of Aden they sailed on for the combined voyage had taken them two weeks until they came into the Arabian Sea having the wind strongly behind them all the way. Two smaller ships, each about 95 feet each, joined them. They were Baghalah, also with lateen sails too. And Solomon waved to them and someone waved back.

Guillaume came out of his cabin and stood with his face directly in the sunlight with his eyes closed. He enjoyed the warmth. Somehow it made thinking easier for him. Perhaps his thinking would show more clarity when he got to India. He had much more time on his hands than he had when he was living in the palace. Guillaume hoped he wasn't wasting his time by going to India. He could only hope for the best. He hated not knowing something and he hated uncertainty.

And the music cut through him again. It had been away for a very long time. He began to tremble, to tingle and the hair on the back of his neck rose when he heard the silent otherworldly sounds. Guillaume staggered around, a crewmember noticed this and came up asking if he was all right. Guillaume grasped the railing to steady himself.

"Yes, I'm fine," he said and patted the back of the man, "yes, I'm all right, even doctors will have a bit of a fever now and again."

The man nodded, but continued to look at him skeptically.

"I'll be okay," said Guillaume defensively.

The crewman slowly went on with his business.

WORRY

Zara looked at the cork sandals Guillaume had sent her a day before he left. She liked them, but put them in her closet with a dozen other pair of shoes men had given her just like the one that Guillaume had given her.

After several weeks when Zara was unable to see Guillaume, she stopped in at his apartment in the palace, but found it occupied by someone else. As she turned around and was about to take her leave of the building she saw a little man in front of her.

"May I help you, Miss?" said Ibn Imran, the Caliph's little man.

"I'm looking for a man named Guillaume de Le Puy, do you know him?" asked Zara.

"Oh, yes, I know him. He sailed back home some time ago, but said he'll probably be back within six months," said the dwarf.

"Oh, six months, that long?" quizzed Zara.

"Yes, he was telling me that he was going to try and practice medicine there but he didn't actually give it too much hope," said the buffoon, "you might check with his brother, he might know more than I do."

"Where does his brother live?" asked the singing girl.

"His brother lives in town down on Physician's Street, the last white house on that block, aren't you Zara his girl?" wondered the wise comedian.

"Yes, I'm his girl and eh, thank you and who are you?" asked Zara.

"My name is Ibn Imran, I'm the court jester among other things."

"Well, thank you, Ibn Imran."

She leaned over shook his hand and nodded her head. Walking out she sauntered past the streaming maroon silk curtain, brushed by a breeze, which caught her on the throat and she flicked it quickly out of her way. Ibn Imran looked out the building's covered walkway at her disappearing into the distance.

Going into the City with her covered and curtained litter she stopped at Physician's Street and then told the men to take her to the end of it. She knocked a few moments later the door was opened by Jacques.

"May I help you, young lady?"

"Yes, my name is Zara, and eh, I used to know Guillaume, do you know how long he's going to be gone?" asked Zara.

"Oh, I don't really know, I haven't had word from him at Montpellier from where he said he was going to write. I've heard nothing and I'm beginning to get worried," said Jacques.

"You've heard nothing?" asked Zara.

"No, I haven't, I think I'll write our parents in Le Puy. Aren't you the lady he saw among the three singing and dancing girls at Hasdai's party?" asked Jacques.

"Yes, that's me, would you let me know if you get an answer?"

"Yes, where can I reach you?"

"Oh, that's all right, I'll reach you," said Zara not wanting to reveal that she had a small house just outside of town and only one serving-girl to help her.

She said she would get back in touch with Jacques in a month's time by mail. She didn't want him to know too much about her.

"Well, then," he said, "I'll wait for your letter."

Zara nodded and turned around, got into her litter and left.

Back in her house she decided that being one of the three best singing-slave girls in Cordoba, she could open up her own school and teach many girls. Zara let it be known that she would teach the finer points of singing, some 4.000 verses, the ways of dance and the subtle art of deceit for beautiful dancing and singing girls. It took a while before she caught on but finally, when she did, she did well. But all this was after she had the child. For she had been pregnant but didn't know it.

One morning in the third month she threw up and knew she had morning sickness. She had sent Jacques a letter inquiring about Guillaume and he replied that he still had no news from home. He did say that there was a naval report from one of the Caliph's patrol ships which he got from Rabi to the effect that on the day Guillaume's commercial ship sailed north another pirate vessel attacked it and was itself sunk by the naval vessel. And of the bodies recovered none answered the description of Guillaume. So there was still hope that eventually Guillaume might be heard of again.

Some days later he heard from home, from his parents who were now also overly worried about Guillaume.

Jacques never received the letter, which Guillaume had sent from Alexandria in Egypt.

After five more months Jacques gave up on Guillaume being alive and began to give up his practice to other physicians. Al-Hakam came by and seeing Jacques asked him if there was any news. He then asked Jacques to stay on at the palace and work for Hasdai drawing and painting new plants which Rabi had showed him.

Jacques replied: "That's kind of you, but no, I can't, I may also be going home, I haven't decided yet just what exactly I'm going to do except to give up my practice here. You see, my brother and I have always been together and if one of us is gone the other feels as though one has been torn apart and is terribly lonely."

He returned the sword Al-Hakam had given Guillaume and gave it back to him telling Al-Hakam there was no news about Guillaume's disappearance in the fight with the pirate ship.

Jacques also spoke with Juan about Gift at Guillaume's former ranch. He didn't want the horse and Juan should keep it until Guillaume came home.

After that Jacques let the house be taken again by the owner and headed for the mountains to join his Sufi friends, the people of the bench.

LOST

The ship seemed to be flying with a strong breeze filling out the sails and bounding up and down on a fast current when Guillaume came out of his cabin. Seeing the pilot near the mate who guided the rudder, Guillaume went up to him.

"With an astrolabe you can find the latitude from an island near where you are sailing," Guillaume said plainly, "on a clear day or night."

"As long as you are not shrouded in fog, and it isn't raining fish, perhaps. But you'll never find the longitude not with that instrument nor any other thing. The problem of longitude is a problem of time for the earth moves round from east to west, through time, and there is nothing, which can accurately measure time. At least not with the accuracy you need at sea. Scholars told you that you could find longitude with an astrolabe? You must, always remember always, to question authority. It might save your life. Oh, these pompous, conceited scholar-bastards, some of them at least."

Thus began Guillaume's training by Solomon in the nautical, theoretical arts and science of practical results in navigation of the open Indian Ocean.

The crewmen treated him as a stranger until one day one of them broke his arm from being hit with a sudden and fast swinging lateen sail. Being a simple fracture rather than going through the skin as a compound fracture would, he was able to pull it in place and bind it up with a spool of gauze to immobilize the arm. Then, because the crew was a man short, Guillaume took the man's place and learned to work with others.

Whenever the sail had to be raised in the morning's daylight a man stepped to a higher place where crewmen could see him and chanted out the verses of an old song. The men together pulled the rope as one with the chant of the last syllable in each line.

Eventually, Guillaume began to gain the crewmen's respect.

When the wind died down and the men had little to do in the afternoons a couple of the blacks who knew how to swim would dive over the side of the ship with a hammer and some twine and hammer the twine into the areas where it leaked. They knew where the leak was coming from by getting into the hold and by bailing the day's leakage out of the ship. As there were no nails in the ship, it was bound with coir twine and with the bounding of the ship the timbers were continually being loosened. This was a four man job, two men diving with chisel and oakum and one man filling up the bucket with bilge water and another throwing the bucket of seawater over the side of the ship. But the blacks didn't mind they were friendly and laughed and their laughter was infectious to one and all and the Africans had a good time doing quickly one of the worst jobs on the ship.

A tarpaulin covered the middle of the deck far below the sails offering protection from the blazing sun and covering from the splashes of seawater that came up on deck. The tarpaulin also prevented the cargo from getting wet and with the ship rolling back and forth the seawater spilled over the side. Here the men relaxed beneath the boiling sun. Some slept and some spoke gently with one another waiting for the next meal or simply waiting for the wind to come up again. Many of the men were Arabs. And some were Indian, one was Chinese and another Malay.

In the evenings when the air was still and humid the crew would take turns taking showers by standing in the throne where they defecated on the side of the ship while another man let the bucket fall from the end of a spar into the ocean and gathering up more seawater, pulling on the end to bring it to the side of the ship and the man and pulling the second cord attached to the tip of the bucket would spill the seawater all over him. And his body lit up with thousands of tiny creatures, which emitted a luminous shine flickering over their bodies.

And then Guillaume's turn came and he too stood still as the seawater began splashing over him and again the tiny sea creatures emitted their illuminations over the skin of his body. He stood there marveling at its illumination looking down at his arms and legs while the crewmen laughed and howled. This was an experience all of them had gone through.

To vary their diets the men put hooks on lines and threw them overboard to catch fish, but nothing was biting and it was so quiet that even whispers could be heard from the front of the ship.

Someone would tell a simple tale of their experiences back home in a village. The Malaysian would tell of famine in his land forcing him to join others in a pirate band to catch and cripple unwary ships. He'd been wounded once in attacking a ship, but the pirates were beaten off and the crew took him into their circle and in gratitude he'd worked with the pilot in explaining just where the pirate ships were laying in ambush and how to avoid them. He became a valued crewmember.

Late that evening when it became so still a group of Arabs got out their musical instruments from below and began to play. Someone called this piece The Ring Song of Andalusia.

While all this was going on Guillaume thought about the Ring Song he had once seen rippling in the breeze mounted on a pole of white silk and black and gold calligraphy, which read: For Allah! It was all he could read in Arabic at the time.

One man began playing the flute and this went on for several minutes, then another person started playing the drums, accompanying the flute. Then someone else began with the oud, accompanying the first two. At last the tambourine and several other instruments joined in an ever increasingly complex music. The music started slowly and gradually turned faster. They all became lost in it.

A young sailor got up and began to dance a bit like a woman, he was slender and tall and moved his buttocks as if he were double-jointed, which was extremely amusing to watch yet fitted perfectly with the music.

The other Arabs began to clap to the music and soon everyone joined them.

After a while the dancer sat down. But the music went on into the night, slowly subtracting one instrument at a time until there was none left.

The pilot and Guillaume had closed their books and sat down to listen and watch as best they could in the light of the celestial stars. With the dawn the music ceased.

Guillaume went to bed, but pilot stayed up. He and the crewmen watched the sun come up at dawn in a brilliant red-fingered sunrise with golden light chasing away the clouds. And the Muslims got out their prayer mats and made the dawn prayer. Then they all fell gently asleep except pilot who stood, thinking.

When later a breeze caught the sail the men decided to rouse to raise the main sail and thus began the new day. The cook was making breakfast-rice again. Just then the fish started pulling and biting the hooks and the men commenced to pull the lines. The fish fell into the boat squirming, twisting and the men took their short clubs and beat them all to death.

Some of the men set to cleaning the fish and throwing the residue overboard and suddenly there were squads of large fish everywhere.

In less than half an hour the well-cooked fish and rice smelled delicious and they all sat down to a wonderful breakfast. Even Guillaume came out of his cabin when he heard the noise and was given something to eat. As tired as he was the meal perked him up.

The men quickly set about cleaning the decks after their meal and soon with the steadily blowing breeze changed to a gathering wind. The ship steadily lurched forward and the waves with splashing foam and sea spray got over the bulkheads of the SeaWolf. Now the full wind pushed the ship along and she was starting to fly, which made the men happy and they chatted contently with one another.

The flying fish they saw were called 'water bats' which were jumping out of the sea. Even Solomon the Jew was pleased with the day.

"Go, SeaWolf, go, my sweet, can you feel it, you're going faster now, but not too fast," said Solomon, "keep her steady men, yes, that's it!"

The ship burst forward with the next greater puffing of the wind. One of the men became a little too exuberant and accidently slipped off the mast and with a yell he fell into the sea. Happily another man saw it, threw him a line, which he grabbed on to and the man on the ship started pulling him in. Soon this man was saved and smiling.

The pilot laughed at not having lost a man on the journey, which would have dampened the spirits of the men.

"Had the man who saved him not been at his post we wouldn't now be laughing," said Guillaume.

"Yes, that's right," commented the pilot.

The days passed. Sometimes the ship was speeding fast ahead or at times slowing to a halt in the doldrums. And in the early evenings Solomon and Guillaume always conversed about navigation.

"We are headed for the Tuluva coast from Sajawan at 7 ½ degrees P.S. to Sindapura. South of Sindapura is Munaibar, or also called Malabr, and its coast as far as the southern cape of India, down to the town of Kulam Mali," said Solomon, "and there we will find the land of black gold, of pepper!"

"Now tell me the times when we can leave and why or do we just leave at any old time we feel like it?" asked the pilot.

"No, when the sun is in Sagittarius in the second half of November and the first half of December, then the monsoon is blowing in the Northeast. And the sea starts getting too rough to sail. Rough seas will sink ships constructed like ours. From the Red Sea it is two months sail, from the Persian Gulf it's six weeks to the Malabar. We trade in December and set sail in January for the hundreds of Nicobar Islands to pick up water and do a little trading with the natives and then to Kalah Bar on the Malasian coast and on through the Malacca Strait, God willing," said Guillaume who was still the very green navigator and slightly nervous in the science.

"And what do you see in the Malacca Straits?" asked Solomon.

"Well, one thing you find are pirates, or rather they will sometimes find you with several boats waiting for you at different places," replied Guillaume who tried to remember everything he had learned so far from the pilot.

"And what do you do?"

"You fry the funny-looking bastards," Guillaume joked.

"Well, you might try scaring them first before the frying begins, and what do you scare them with?" laughed Solomon.

"Eh, well, you spray them with Greek fire from our Arab marines," said Guillaume.

"No, that is not correct. And when do you give the order?" asked Solomon.

"When, eh, not until the ships are very close," said Guillaume, "you never show them your best hand not until last when it is too late for the enemy."

"Just before they throw their spears you give the order to fire the crossbows, which may set them back a little. But what will really get their attention is your 'frying' them, and the result of all this discussion is that I'm putting you in charge of that part of the operation."

"Me?" said Guillaume.

"Yes, why not, it's part of the job, your job. You've got to learn it sooner or later," said the pilot.

"Why me," asked Guillaume in an anxious voice.

"Why not you?" the pilot shrugged his shoulders. "I'll turn the ship over to you and I'll just go into my cabin and lay down and get a little rest and let you slay your little dragons. Of course, if they have crossbows and shoot you first, well, I'll have to wake up anyway, come out and take control of the crew, win the battle and sail on through the strait. We'll bury you when we have a chance, well, at least before you turn black and begin stinking, but then, I'll have lost my sleep and you know how much I love my rest, how irritable I am when I've not gotten my complete sleep which by the way I never can on a voyage."

Guillaume puked himself silly over the railing on the side of the ship. And the pilot laughed at Guillaume's discomfort, slapping him hard on the back. Then he felt a little sorry for the young man. He went into his cabin for a moment and came back with a damp cloth and gave it to Guillaume to wipe himself with.

"Think. If you're lucky enough to be alive to remember the smell of burning flesh for the rest of your life then you'll thank God that it wasn't you who was burned," said Solomon.

"I guess we can skip the rest of the evening's navigation, don't you think?" The pilot remarked and began laughing again.

And the sun slipped below the horizon turning the clouds bright orange, then bright red glowing ever darker until they turned gray changing into the black streaks.

The Muslims spread their prayer mats on the ship for Al-Maghreb. The crew simply watched as the sun's golden chariot flamed into the West slowly disappearing below the horizon. And the ship's lamp was lit.

And so the days wore on. Something different happened every day to make each day unique. One of the men carved wood with several small special knives, sometimes a flying horse with one leg on a pedestal or a large bird with wings extended and sometimes a ship with a full-breasted sail. He was very fast and accurate.

A few of the Arabs who could play music would sometimes practice. And some read the Qur'an. Guillaume would listen to the men recite and then he too, would go and read his bible late into the night and then last of all, he got down on his knees and prayed and confessed his sins to Almighty God.

Solomon, the pilot navigator too would study and pray and recite to God in his Jewish way.

The Persian captain would enjoy another suck on his opium pipe and his dreams would allow him to slip far away on fantasy clouds.

In the days following the night of prayer in which they felt the gray fogged ghosts of the jinn beginning to swarm around them, and trying to ignore them or what they thought they could see and hear they spoke quietly to one another about what lay ahead. One of the men looked up and could see the lamps lit on the other ships, one on each side to the back and another lamp in front on each side.

"Do you know that the pepper of Malabar is so much better than that of Malacca?" said the pilot quietly continuing their conversation.

"No," said Guillaume quietly.

"Do you know what the word Malabar means?" asked Solomon.

"No," replied Guillaume.

"It means land of pepper."

Guillaume nodded his head.

"And we are sailing towards Sandabur near Chandrapur, on the island of Sindapura," said Solomon with a touch of conceit.

"Yes."

"Do you feel the fog coming down on you like a giant black carpet?"

"Yes, I do."

"I think it's time to wake up the crew for they appear to be sleeping or are becoming mentally paralyzed as a result of the fog," reasoned Solomon. "Wake up, men, wake up!"

He clapped his hands sharply and some of the men began to rouse and shake their sleep away.

"Come on, let's show a little activity, let's dance and that includes me," laughed Solomon.

And the men languorously got up and started to follow Solomon. Most of the men felt foolish, some of them were jumping up and down, throwing out their arms in an awkward fashion while others laughed. A few men looked and danced in a similar way to the women temple dancers of Bali, which made Guillaume frown. They rotated their wrists and heads to the side while swinging their hips in some manner like the women, but entirely without finesse.

"All right now, you, come here, you'll be the leader and I want you to dance, and one of you others, go and get some musical instruments and play a tune, any tune will do." said Solomon. "And we shall dance like the beauties of the islands!"

At that the men all laughed and it got their chests heaving a little.

"No, no, no," said Solomon at the top of his voice. "You've got it all wrong, you must do it together."

They all tried.

"That's right, now you've got it, alright, now we swing our hips, yes, like the leader," he chuckled.

All the men were completely awake now and after a few minutes the pilot let the men go back to their routines this time with renewed vigor.

And the men began to sing songs of far away locations, of loneliness and of finding love. They stayed at their posts until dawn when the sun began to peak and light their darkened sky.

They raised the main sail and caught the wind further. Now everyone was working hard to give the ship its head and let it fly like a bird.

In the days, which followed, Guillaume began to feel homesick. He felt he had thrown everything away that gave his life meaning: his work and parents, his brother Jacques, Zara. Not to forget his friends Rabi and prince Al-Hakam, his music and library. Everything, which meant something to him, his entire world was turned over. And he felt very lonely.

Guillaume's world now revolved around this ship, the SeaWolf, and it was sailing toward India. He was smashing through time into a new future in which he had little control. He had everything in the world going for him and he had thrown it all away for what? He could have stayed at the palace and continued to practice his profession and eventually become a full physician, while there in all the comforts accorded to an assistant doctor. But no, he had to do what he was doing. Perhaps he could have quit the Benedictines and married Zara or someone else? Cordoba was the perfect city, a City of Light, a city worth staying in, worth living and working in. And the libraries of Al-Hakam, he could have virtually lived in those libraries.

He was beginning to like the work, to adapt to it and look forward to it in the morning. Guillaume could feel the pull of his arm muscles as they expanded and his stomach began to tighten up. And his leg muscles as well. He was becoming comfortable with the ship. He and the crew had finally become part of the ship.

In the evening the clouds were brilliant with whites shading into pinks and reddened maroons and the light in the sky gradually dimmed and the sun disappeared from sight.

That night the Arabs again brought out their musical instruments and began to play.

The melodies made everyone feel better and the laughing and banter went on until the darkness of night was upon them. No one felt the foggy grip of the Jinn.

In the morning a man's arm was badly slashed. It all came about as two men who had been playing with their sharpened knives were thrown off balance and one man accidently hit the other man's arm. Guillaume got his medical kit and washed the blood off so he could see the damage. Two other men had to hold the injured man down due to his acute pain. When Guillaume saw the gash he washed the man's arm with a little alcohol and soothed it with an ointment. Then he began to sew it up and gave the man a little opium. The man would sleep very well tonight, thought Guillaume, at least letting the intensity of the pain diminish.

The pilot having seen all this nodded to himself. He was glad for having gotten a good ship's doctor on board, one who could help out during emergencies with the ship's crew. He knew he'd chosen correctly.

Still with two men absent from work, Guillaume had more than enough to handle. It would be several days before the man with the broken arm could begin helping out, and the one with the slashed arm would be useless perhaps for as long as a month.

In the morning the sea swells were quite strong and sometimes swirling round. They would catch them at sixes and sevens and tip the huge ship nearly over. Frantically the crew went to work and pilot had a stern face on him.

The wind picked up, the pilot ordered the men to raise sails before they lost them and broke the main mast. The tarpaulin cover began tearing. The men didn't have a chance to do anything except slide and fall with the rising and falling of the ship. It was a miracle that no one was lost. The men tied ropes around them and attached them to a railing where they worked, but it was useless for the ship was being tossed this way and that.

Even pilot became alarmed and took over the tiller releasing the man for work with the crew. The squall hit them broadside with a tremendous crash and literally moved the ship sideways several feet across the waves. What the other two ships had to contend with was unimaginable. But the smaller ships were much more nimble in the sea than the larger one and they had no leaks.

And then the bottom of the world fell out from under them and anyone who wasn't tied down slipped backward toward the cabins and slammed into the teak woodwork with such a great and devastating force that the air was knocked completely out of them. They thought they were in a maelstrom, now the sails were ripping out on the mizzens.

Then suddenly, just as the wind and seas became angry, they were relaxing into a peaceful and quiet sea. The men stood in their positions while all this was going on thinking that the hailstorm would begin anew. Then they heard the thunder. Grey-black ugly and swirling clouds came rolling in from the horizon, then lightening hit upon them all round. It was bluish-green and one flash it hit the top of the large mast. A cone of transparent light came down the mast and crackled at them. In sheer heart-stopping fright they scrambled back from it, but it was too late. The lightening caught a man in his head whose breathing stopped suddenly. Then there was more thunder. The sailors tried their best to revive him but could not. They experienced their first casualty.

Lightening flashed hit again where they were. Again thunder crashed near by. And further slashes of electricity momentarily whitened the skies. Then there was complete darkness, followed by lightening again. It went on and on.

The next day they wrapped the dead man well and weighted him down with blocks of lead tied to some of the unraveling ropes in the morning's light, saying a simple prayer to Allah that he would swiftly go to paradise. And then they dropped him gently into the Indian Ocean and watched his body sink quickly into the deep indigo water.

Nearly everyone was morose for the next few days. No one wanted to do much talking. The gayness was gone now and with it the laughing banter. From now on it was all work getting to India. At this point they were three men short, and the work became increasingly frustrating and tiring. But they pushed on.

In the evening when the night sky began to manifest the man at the front of the ship noticed something, got up and ran to the main mast. He shimmied up the polished wood like a monkey until he reached the top and looked out.

"The sea is glowing," he called out. "Yes, the sea is glowing. There is a blue-green sea monster out there."

Some of the men had gathered around the front of the ship looking outward and they too could see what lay ahead. They saw a glowing greenish blue foaming sea. For several moments the men simply stood there waiting and watching the ship coming closer and closer to that faint glow. Suddenly, they were in it, the light increased, from the sea or the monster.

A few moments later a man was running along the topside of the ship and then down into it and returned with the Qur'an and then read certain sections for their protection in this worrisome situation. And with every moment it became progressively darker and the lower light of the sea became brighter and brighter.

One of the men fashioned a corded rope tied to the mast and had knots coiled into it and wrapped it around his body. Then he climbed up on the railing and using the rope as a brace began walking down the side of the ship into the foam. He even went under the seawater.

When he came up he started to scream and yet he wasn't hurt. He simply could see under water! Some of the men were frightened and began reciting Ayat Al-Kursi, the Qur'an's Throne Verse.

Solomon had been watching the men sizing them up as it were, and said nothing but simply watched. Guillaume watched him and then the men and then the glowing sea like churning milk. Only this "milk" glowed.

"You know what this is, don't you?" asked Guillaume.

"Yes, I surely do, I've seen it before, many times," said the pilot.

"What is it then?"

"Your guess is as good as mine, my young friend."

"I suppose you've seen many strange things in the sea?"

"Yes, many things, in the sea, on the sea and over it, too, but of all of them this is one of the most remarkable and unusual, and I don't know what it is, but I know this, it won't hurt anyone or the ships. It is as if the seawater is alive rolling and glowing as if it had a strange life of its own."

We stood there watching and looking at it until we became sleepy. But this was different from the white glowing foam we'd seen previously as the ship cut its way through the sea.

In the morning they threw out their fishing lines again hoping for some fresh fish, but there were no bites.

One day we felt a very large bump, a number of the crew fell over and saw great black fishes diving into the sea and up again and down blowing the air through their blowholes. Solomon sent someone down to the bilges to report if more water than usual had gotten inside the ship, but that wasn't the case. The pilot ordered a crewman to climb the main mast and look for ambergris, a kind gray lumpy matter, which these giant fishes sometimes coughed up and then it floated on the seawater. It was very valuable and made into perfumes. But the crewman saw nothing and the fish moved away.

Guillaume wasn't feeling well and he stumbled back into his cabin. The next day the pilot came and tried to rouse him. Guillaume stirred, but was unable to get up for he was very ill. The best thing was to allow Guillaume to sleep.

For several days Guillaume tossed and turned in his bed, and then one day his fever broke and he slowly got up, dressed and went outside to the deck. He was staggered into another sailor. But someone came up behind him, who knew Guillaume would fall, and he did. The crewman caught Guillaume's arm and pulled him over to a chair in front of his cabin. Guillaume tried to look up, but he was still fainting and coming back to consciousness. The crewman tied Guillaume to his chair just enough to keep him from falling off. Solomon saw this and nodded. In an hour or so Guillaume began to come around fully and was able to take a little water. Later he was given a warm light soup and as he finished it he looked up at the crewman and thanked him for what he did.

"It is nothing, don't worry, just get well so you can treat us when we're ill," he chuckled, "we help one another, eh?"

And Guillaume was able to give a weak smile and look up at the man. But presently his head dropped back down again and he passed out.

The crewman said to the pilot: "I think he will be alright, soon."

"Yes," he said, "in time."

The ship began to pick up a little speed and the men instantly cheered up at now having something to do. Even Guillaume raised his head and looked a bit less white, but he was still panting through his mouth.

The wind came from behind and brushed his cheeks waking him up.

Solomon gave him a drink of water and this revived him even more. And then the pilot untied his cords and Guillaume again thanked him.

After twilight Solomon took him to his cabin and laid him gently down as if he were his own son.

"Thank you Solomon," whispered Guillaume who promptly went to sleep.

The pilot quietly closed the door on his way out.

The men began to feel the warmth of the climate change and they knew they were getting close to India, even though it was still a way to go.

In the morning Guillaume staggered out of his cabin and almost fell into Solomon who caught him, steadied him and sat him down in the chair. Guillaume's voice was now stronger.

"I'm better," he said.

"Look, to the East, over there, that, my friend, is Al-Hind. Do you see it?"

"No, I don't see anything."

The pilot was a very strong man and he picked up the chair in which Guillaume sat and swung him around to the eastern-most position, towards the Malabar Coast.

"Can you see it now?"

"Ah, yes, yes, I can."

Solomon said nothing but indicated with his gestures to the crew. They already knew what to do and they turned the sails closer to the East. The pilot had the first mate turn the rudder into the direction of the wind and the middle of the ship. Once this was done the wind from the west came up and pushed them with a full and ballooning rush, which the men could all feel for the ship suddenly went a bit faster cutting the waves a little higher and slowly rocking back and forth a little deeper into the Indian Ocean. The SeaWolf was going nearly as fast as she could into the evening's twilight.

They dropped six anchors and furled the sails. The other ships also stopped and dropped their anchors as well.

After the morning's prayers they pulled anchors and unfurled the sails, which set them to travel gently down the coast. Solomon knew the land and the landscape like the back of his hand, every nook and cranny, of every hill and inlet, and every ridged coastline or flat beach for several hundred leagues behind him and forward.

By midday the pilot found what he had been looking for: a network of waterways, inlets from the sea and lagoons. There was the sandy beach beside the inlets into Kerala, close to the palatial home of the Raja.

As the tide came out in the morning they had to wait until evening before the tide went back in, and they went with a burst of speed having backed off until they had a good distance between themselves, and the shore. And on they went straight onto the flat sandy beach, where they began unloading the ship to lighten her so they could get her back end up in the air and on to the grooved sawhorses they would put under her. For the ships needed nearly a month to be refurbished and once the ship had dried out it would be swabbed on the inside with mops dipped in vegetable oil all across the inside, bottom and the outside had to be smeared with a mixture of waterproof lime and tree gum, which they carried in boxes in the ship.

By the afternoon they had unloaded her of all the goods they would trade there. One of the other boats also came in and beached, but it didn't need any grooved sawhorses to hold it up as the ship was used for emergencies in case the larger ship was damaged or lost and to carry a fourth of the full load. It too unloaded all the goods it had in her.

The smaller ship was used to navigate the narrowed inland sea waters between the elongated islands.

Waving goodbye to the other ship they began snaking down to the large inlet, which led directly to the Maharajah's magnificent palace. This was all new territory for Guillaume. They floated through blue lagoons and Solomon walked up behind him and pointed out the different trees; cashews, bananas, mango trees, nutmegs and bread fruit, papaya and jack fruits and palms everywhere along the canal.

After about ten leagues they came out into a rather large river flooded by the monsoon rains. Everything was so green and shaded by palm trees and bamboo and it was cool and humid compared to the hot days and nights on the sea. Two of the men poled the channels to hurry them up for the wind was dying a bit.

The western mountains lay in front of them a great number of leagues off while they made about five leagues per hour. Now and then they could see a few pepper vines snaking up trees. By the time it started getting dark they came up to the palace and docked at steps cut in stone many years ago. The palace was lit up and someone came running out to greet us, it turned out to be a servant.

"Welcome! Yes, you can dock right there, just tie up the boat," he said, "how are you, we haven't seen you for a long time."

"Oh, I'm fine, thank you so much. Yes, it's been a long time since I was here last. I've brought with me a few guests of mine, crewmen and my captains and my doctor," said the pilot.

They walked up the gently rising slope to the palace. It was a tropical environment. The Raj came out onto the porch and met the visitors in the friendliest way.

"Welcome, I haven't seen you for a long time!"

"Yes, it's good to see you again, my friend."

"Come on in, come on in, we're going to have a very large feast for you."

"Well, you don't have to trouble yourself on account of us," said pilot.

"No, trouble at all! And how have you been these last two years?"

"Well, very well, and you haven't changed a bit."

The men talked about many things after their required greeting ritual was over, the weather, business and how good it was and how it was getting better, how the Raj had collected 42 from 40 percent of the pepper harvest.

"That's wonderful," said Solomon.

INDIA

Two very beautiful nut brown young women were standing in front of a floor-length mirror, giggling, with their hands on their hips and being completely naked. Then they both moved, swinging their hips. And they laughed uproariously. The princess had on a necklace with a stone pendent. Her companion and maid also had on a necklace, which had a stone on the end of it. But the stones were quite different. One was the Koh-i-Noor, the Mountain of Light, and the other was made of glass, shaped exactly like the one of the princess. The women in the family passed the stone down from mother to daughter as there was a curse on men owning the diamond. The princess' mother had died the previous year. The diamond was given at that time to the princess to own and wear. She placed it between the ample breasts of a particularly over-developed sixteen-year old girl.

"I wonder if he'll look at me or at my diamond, or both?" stated princess Gayatri. "If he looks at the diamond there will be no rustle in his trousers."

At that, they both broke up again with high-pitched screams of laughter.

"I don't know Gayatri but, he is, oh, so handsome, you should have seen his red beard!" said her companion, the maid. "I also know he is a good doctor and he's tall."

While listening, the princess picked up off the floor a red dress with bands of yellow, orange, green, and silver and gold worked into it. She put it on. The young women both had long black hair and had already put on their pearl earrings, makeup, and a dash of perfume: on their wrists and between their breasts and on the shoulders some amber and patchouli on the neck and cheeks. A touch of musk had been placed on their abdomen and sandalwood on their thighs. They also put on their anklet bangles with various red rubies, black opals and pearls, and golden bracelets on their arms. Lastly they put on their golden-green colored blouses and red leather sandals and rings.

Every night that there were men coming to their palatial home it was special to them, no matter how often it happened. But tonight was extra special because a tall, white-skinned with a red headed foreigner had arrived who couldn't speak a word of their language: Malayalam.

The princess swirled round and around clock-wise then suddenly stopped while her dress continued turning. And wham, she threw her arms out; her right arm extended upward and her left extended outwardly.

"Ha!" she said.

And her friendly companion laughed. Finally she, too, got dressed in nearly identical clothing and swirled round and round. They shook their heads letting their full long, black, satin hair unfurl and watched themselves in the mirror.

Now both of them danced several steps of the sacred dance twisting their arms and wrists and fingers into various positions and nodding and bobbing their heads left and right of which only Indian girls are able to do. They were rolling their eyes up and around and down, as if they were on stage telling a story with body movements. They danced to an unheard raga.

The music ensemble that would perform later had came down from the North with their sitars, their tablas, the veena flute, and a long double-headed drum. The young women danced and danced for several minutes in anticipation of the music they would hear that night. They would dance to the music of the great soul breaking

Matanga, one of the finest musicians in all of India.

Guillaume was listening as the pilot was conversing with the Raj of the Malabar Coast. He presented Guillaume as the ship's doctor. The Raj nodded at him and Guillaume nodded back. A moment later the Raj raised his hand crooked his index finger, and the loveliest woman Guillaume had seen in a long time came over and her father presented his only daughter, Gayatri, to the men. Guillaume looked at her with curious eyes, and saw the size of the stone she wore around her neck then he quickly looked her over without becoming too obvious about it.

Gayatri smiled at Guillaume letting her eyes take him in. She said something in a foreign tongue to the effect that he was welcome anytime to visit their country and her father's home. Then she turned and walked back to sit next to the music ensemble. The musicians began tuning up their instruments and this was a sign they were ready to begin and that the host and guests should become quiet and seated.

The musicians began a slow moving piece, an evening raga, with Gayatri performing very slowly and gracefully a moving dance dedicated to God. The music produced a hypnotic feeling in Guillaume and an impression of timelessness within the eternal vistas of India he had momentarily witnessed. It was a feeling of something he'd never felt before.

There were slow moving cattle tilling the fields with a farmer behind them, walking ever so slowly and rhythmically over a hot landscape with hardly a breath of fresh air except along the coast. The coastal lands were raised islands of tree roots with large flowering trees canopied and shading the waterways where fresh grasses grew amongst the little soil that rested in them in between the cool estuaries. The scenario sheltered their ships well and the men found they could walk easily on the floating islands.

Through the effect of the music Guillaume felt the timelessness of life, something he had never sensed before. The girl sang as well as she danced. It was the dance of the celestial enchantress, known for graceful almost seductive movements. When the end of the melody came she quickly sat down. Guillaume was entranced.

Waiters asked the guests what they would like to eat and when they got to Guillaume he said he'd have what the pilot was having and the pilot said he'd have what the Raj was having.

Then they all sat down and dined on a wonderful tasty and spicy meal. There was more music. This time it was dinner background music. The host and the guests quietly spoke with one another. The second dancer began her performance. Guillaume was intrigued with it.

The Raj didn't knew any Arabic, so only Solomon could understand Malayalam, as well as Arabic, and Ladino, which was the language the Jews spoke among themselves. The pilot was a rather versatile man, a man of no vices or faults. For Guillaume nothing was too much to say of Solomon, the pilot.

"You see, Gayatri, my daughter," said the Raj to his guests, "isn't all that good, and one of the reasons for that is that she is my daughter. Some day she will become queen of this realm and won't have time to devote to being a temple dancer. It was simply a discipline and any discipline will do to teach her the responsibilities of a monarch."

"Interesting," stated Solomon.

"She started her training aged six and now she's sixteen so she's been at it for only ten years. A truly good dancer would have been at it for five more years than her and they would put their best efforts into it for it was either temple dancing or marriage to a no-body or the streets. And being a temple dancer is looked upon as a very high position in our society. So these young women must be shapely, have patience, incredible patience, always be friendly, be able to take orders, as well as giving them and learn all the basic moves and steps of sacred dance particularly the Kathakali. It is a theatrical dance from Kerala where she dances an episode from the Ramayana and Mahabharata and their meanings and they must look and be beautiful. We consider dance as the pulsating rhythm of cosmic life and Indians have always practiced it as a sacred means of entering into divine consciousness."

"Tell us some more, if you would be so kind dear Raj," said the pilot.

"Yes, the purpose of the dance is to release the countless souls of mankind from the snares of illusion, and the place of dance is in their hearts. And the center of the universe is within the heart.

The waiters were now serving the dessert to all the guests.

"We even have books on sacred dancing."

Then pilot turned around to his left and always translated for Guillaume what the Raj had to say, with Guillaume listening and nodding.

"Here in Kerala, in southwest India, the Kathakali dance style is indigenous to this area because villagers perform for other villagers for the sake of God. The dancers are trained, very well trained," said the Raj.

To the sound of another evening raga they all slowly enjoyed every tiny taste of the dessert and let their taste buds in on the secret of Indian delicacies.

A few moments later Guillaume thought his tongue was on fire. And he started grabbing for the cooling drink placed to his right. The dining went on for a long time.

After a while, Guillaume had to get up and go for a short walk, as he was still dizzy and weak from his recent feverish illness. He went outside from the host's mansion into his garden and in the cool breezes, which flooded the garden with perfumed scents. Guillaume sat down on a wall made out of stones and enjoyed the garden in the early evening's light which was changing. He thought he heard a rustling in the bushes in the garden. But there was no one there.

He smelled the faint perfume of jasmine in the air. There were many scents in the garden. Every bush it seemed had a new fragrance, an aroma. Then he heard the tinkling of tiny bells and two cool hands put themselves over his eyes. He quickly turned around to see Gayatri standing beside him and laughing gently. Guillaume chuckled. The young woman clasped his hands in her own and put Guillaume's hands up on her shoulders, and she bent back closing her eyes and slightly puckered her mouth. Guillaume kissed her on the cheek and she frowned.

She stepped closer to him. Feeling his body against hers. And Guillaume became nervous. She laughed and took the man's role in hunting for the pleasures of lust. Putting his hand on her breast he felt her pulsating breath on his shoulder, and slowly withdrew his hand. Then he put his hands on her shoulders forcing her to turn around and to step back a bit. And he looked into her green eyes, which stared at him questioningly. She leaned her head and looked at him again.

It came to Guillaume that she merely wanted to play at love for the sake of pleasure alone. He imagined that this young women might have had done this many times before. So, he kissed her on her mouth, turned her around and slapped her behind while pushing her away. He shook his head and smiled. She didn't understand that he didn't want to become one of her conquests and she became angry and in a huff walked away leaving Guillaume where he was.

Gayatri believed she had felt with her leg a rustling in his trousers.

Guillaume stayed outdoors for nearly an hour before thinking of going in to rejoin the feast of the Raj. He was pondering about his future. He thought she had certainly found out that after all he was very human. Guillaume found himself suspended, or at least he thought he was, in roughened purgatory somewhere between heaven and hell. The air was humid, and sweet, and many of the blossoms had folded up, it was becoming quite late before he decided to go back in.

When he had already made the decision to go in something came upon him subtly and delicately, a feeling, which he was compelled to go with whether he wanted to or not. So he leaned his back against the low wall and the music suddenly went through him again this time very hard making his hand come up with his palm open as if he were about to gesture.   While the music continued in his mind he was thinking that whenever a man wants to say something and his tongue gets all tied up in knots he knows that at that instant he must turn to music as one of the ways in which he can express himself.

He seemed to think that he could add color to the music itself for each color had a sound, a certain note to it, a certain feeling in it, and the colors moved and intertwined with one another to make brilliantly colorful-sound symphonies to match anything he could possibly imagine in his mind.

And every way he turned there was light, as he had never known before.

Guillaume was suddenly tired, it had been a long day and it was time to go to sleep. He would sleep well that night for he was exhausted. And so he got up, and went back inside the Raj's palace.

The Raj and the pilot were sitting in the large room. The Raj was telling Solomon about his valley.   Tigers, deer and many mammals native to the South such as the

Malabar giant squirrel, and lion-tailed Macaque, and Civet mongoose, from which a substance with a consistency of butter or honey was taken from the anal glands of the mammal as a stabilizing agent in a perfume made for men called musk. Sometimes they would cook the animal. It was a great delicacy. There were also medicinal plants there such as Neelakurinji, which blooms only once in every twelve years.

Intrigued by what the Raj said, Solomon readily agreed to going on his hunt, automatically inviting Guillaume and the captains of the other ships.

"Good," said the Raj, "we'll leave tomorrow, at the break of dawn!"

With their spears, shields, crossbows, and daggers the fully armed men trolled through the tall grass at the entrance to the valley while their porters with all their equipment followed.

Breaking the grass released the fine odor and in the distance they heard what they were looking for: the growl of a tiger. But they could not see the animal over the grasses. Coming out of the old marsh they walked up to a low lying region in mud flats where hundreds of butterflies stood taking up water.

Guillaume stepped gently into the flats and immediately was surrounded by various colored butterflies, which clung to his clothing. He looked up at the other men and smiled. Then with a sudden breeze they all flew away. A crow pheasant flew up and away, then a Hoopoe. But the men had not brought their falcons with them and weren't hunting birds. They went on and carefully walked down again into another marshy area, one foot at a time, for this area was known to harbor tigers who attacked men using the tall grass as a cover.

With their spears raised and shields in front of them they slowly went through the grasses, and men with crossbows came next. But coming to the end of the marsh they found nothing.

Again, walking up and out of the marshy area they decided to wait for the late afternoon sun, as it was rather hot by now. The porters began to set up camp. The Raj instructed some of the porters to barbeque a bit of meat, which might entice the tiger to come closer to the men with their advantage of high ground, as well as feeding the men as well. But it too, was to no avail, not today.

This next day the men strode out and down with an easy gait onto the plain. They had all stopped to drink water from their gourds. The porters too had put down their burdens. And the Raj cautioned the porters to come closer to the main group.

"This tiger, I think I've known from before. It's a very smart and cautious one. We will have to go to him, but to trap him in a place where he wants us to be, we shall have to be very careful with him or he will play with us at his advantage, tiring us out and when we're tired, springs his trap," said the Raj.

They went on and on into the late afternoon. The sun was now in their eyes. Not so for the tiger. His eyes always looked westward at what was tracking him. He settled down in a low-lying area below a rise in the ground just where the hunting party couldn't see him. But something in him made him growl quietly and he rose up, and with a last look took off around the trackers and slipped in behind them. The tiger hadn't urinated in the low-lying area to mark his outer boundary. The Raj and one of his expert trackers still were able to smell the animal.

"I think he's gone behind us now," said the tracker.

"You are probably correct, hurry up, you don't want to be the tiger's dinner, do you?" said the Raj.

The men in the back began running up the hill as fast they could with all the heavy equipment they were carrying. They were all completely out of breath by the time they had gotten to the top.

"Yes, he's outwitted us this day, but tomorrow is another day!"

"Well, I think he's got the day for it's getting late, too late to be going for him in the grass," judged the Raj.

"Yes, I think so too," replied the tracker.

One of the men slipped and fell on the ground and right there almost in broad daylight the tiger rose, growled, and suddenly turned and took off into the grasses before any of the men could open their mouths or react.

"He's telling us he feels quite comfortable in showing himself to us just when we were caught out of readiness for him, this one is going to take some thinking to get him," said the tracker. "This won't be the trick of a goat on a leash, while we hide in waiting for him."

219

"No," said the Raj, "he's making it interesting for us, isn't he?"

"I think he's going to lead us on a goose chase," laughed the tracker.

"You could very well be right," chuckled the Raj.

"We might as well get a fire started for protection."

Some of the men started to pitch tents and others made a fire digging a large shallow ditch, and placing rocks around the outside ring. Others still began picking up loose branches and sticks, breaking them into smaller pieces. Guillaume looked at the flora in the area, yet he kept close to the men and equipment.

Solomon and the Raj settled down into a conversation.

"What do you think this tiger will do next, Raj?" asked the pilot.

"I think there are three or more possibilities. The first is that he will run away. Second, he could just keep doing what he has been doing, which is not probable. This tiger never does the same thing twice. Third, he can do something unusual for a tiger. For example, he could hide in a densely packed tree waiting for us, and knowing his first attack will be his last. But, somehow, I just don't think that is possible, or even remotely probable. Or he could hide and watch what we're doing and where we're going, waiting for us to slip up by allowing a man to fall too far behind all the others, then, he leaps. I don't know, we'll just have to wait and see," said the Raj.

"I'm afraid I'm out of my element, except when I'm buying and selling or trading," said Solomon.

The men had had their dinner, the evening came on quickly, and the fire burned low. It was time to prepare for bed. One of the porters threw a few of the larger logs on the fire and the fire gradually took hold of them. It burned the outer bark off of them, shooting off little gas jets from the bark and crackles of heat expanding the wood loudly and splitting the silence of the men.

When the log fire had burned down the porter leveled the bright yellow and reds of hot ashes until the undulating heat stirred back up again into a flame. But then the porter became drowsy and let his head fall downward and quickly jerked it back up again. He wasn't supposed to sleep and had to guard the encampment and keep the fire going.   The man slapped his face hard several times to keep himself awake and took a drink from his gourd. He also had a little extra bit to eat from the barbecue and this seemed to revive him somewhat.

Within half an hour he was back to dropping his head again in his efforts to remain awake.   Then he stood up and walked around the fire feeling the warmth on his legs. The tiger waited, watching the man as he walked around the fire and finally sat down.

At last the tiger ingested the air in large gulps, got himself ready to spring but then settled down again and slowly came closer to the man like a cat getting ready to kill a bird. The tiger was using the foliage partly for cover and partly to leave as little of himself as possible for the victim to see. He was now out in the open just a few yards away from the man, watching the man breathe and listening to the other men's breathing all around him. It was very quiet. The wind blew gently toward the animal. The tiger instinctively knew he would have to act fast. He wouldn't have much time but to kill the man with a bite from his strong jaws and run leaping into the night. The tiger was a master of patience, stealth, and stalking. He was guided by hatred. Men had hunted him before many times.

The tiger suddenly leaped on the man biting him deeply in the neck and killing him instantly. And before the men could wake up and arm themselves the tiger began to move off.

Only one of them raised an armed crossbow, but another man bumped into him in fright. The man fired prematurely at the tiger and having missed hit another man in the leg. Everything happened so fast that in an instant it was over.

Guillaume was up and out of his tent in a flash, but not fast enough to gather a spear or crossbow and fire at the animal. The wounded porter wailed. So Guillaume got out his kit and went to the man seeing that the arrow had gone all the way through him. The porter sat on the ground and cried, he was grimacing and squeezing his leg near the punctured arrow. Guillaume grabbed his arm. Another man came up and Guillaume told the man to hold the wounded man's wrist, while Guillaume fished around in his kit for a short rope, which he tied into a noose and slipped around the man's right hand. Then Guillaume found his bottle and slipped his finger into the man's cheek with some opium on the end of it. He massaged the man's gums to get it into him and after a little while the man fainted.

Guillaume took cutters from inside his kit, and snapped the arrow, which had the feather on it out, leaving the arrow in the wound to prevent bleeding for a moment. He then took another bottle of alcohol, took off the stopper and placed it on the ground. Guillaume took out some bandages and gauze, wrapping it up into halves each time and took another and did the same. Then he pulled the arrow out and with his other hand poured the alcohol on both sides of the wound and then he wrapped the bandage around it, placing the gauze under the bandage as he wrapped and wrapped. Then he placed a small stick under the bandage and twisted it, and then he put another bandage around the stick so it couldn't move and prevented the man from bleeding to death.

Then once he was done a small number of men lifted the body and placed him on a blanket. The men then took two poles they had from the tents and pierced the blanket a foot down from the edge, placing the pole at the end and began turning the blanket around the pole until the blanket came to the hole at which point Guillaume took a small string and put it through the blanket and around the pole, tying it and then taking another string and putting it in the middle of the side of the blanket, tying it and another further string and putting it at the end of the blanket, tying it and the man was ready to be carried home.

For now everyone had to go back home. They felt depressed for it seemed as though the hunt was completely unsuccessful. Guillaume never looked for medicinal plants and herbs, as he was one of those looking out for the tiger on the way out and watching over the injured man. They also knew they would have to be careful now, because the tiger had made so bold a move.

The wounded man groaned, as he was being tossed and turned by the porters over uneven ground. But it couldn't be helped. At least the arrow had not struck the bone and chipped or broken it, the man would recover. In the meantime he would be miserable.

Just in time they brought the man into the Raj's palatial home. The Indian doctor said it looked like something done by a professional. And Guillaume smiled.

"Where are you from, young doctor?"

"I am from the Mediterranean on the far northern side to the West, from Frankland," said Guillaume.

"I didn't know there were any doctors from that part of the world."

"There are a few, but mostly they are herbalists and not doctors or physicians as in the Arab sense of the word."

"But you, you are a physician, or at least a doctor how do you account for that?"

"The Caliph Abd Ar-Rahman III Al-Nasir is known for his generosity!"

"Ah, really?"

"Yes."

"Did you hear the news that he died?"

"What?"

"He's dead! Yes, and Al-Hakam II is now on the throne."

"It happens to the best of us, one day we will all die."

"By the way, how and why did you get all the way out here to India?"

"One of the reasons was that I had heard of the story of Alexander the Great when I was in Cordoba. And another was about a Persian physician, who translated some animal fables, and the piece was translated into Arabic. It was entitled Kalila wa Dimna, and he had originally gone to India where he heard these tales. In any case the Persian physician was supposed to have been in search of powerful herbs that grow in the mountains there and he met some Indian sages, who explained that this legend is but an allegory: the mountains are wise men, the herbs their books, and the dead the ignorant of the earth. Apparently, he was happy with this explanation and returned to Persia and presented a large number of books he had translated to the great King Khusraw. He kept practicing his profession and lived in despair because he couldn't prevent his patients from dying. That's all I know. I came to India for the purpose of finding new or better medicines."

The Indian doctor looked impressed.

"Actually I was on my way to visit home, traveling by ship when a pirate came upon us, attacked out ship and set fire to it while it sank. I tried to help save the ship and killed one of the pirates. But an arrow from a crossbow hit me in the upper left hand side of the chest and knocked me down and out of the ship onto a slat of wooden boards, barely enough to carry my body. Unknown to me a captain and a pilot on another ship came upon me and saved my life. The arrow was taken out of my shoulder. Then I woke up on board of their ship outside of Alexandria on the opposite side of the Mediterranean. Not where I needed to go. The captain told me he had a cousin who had a very large ship docked at the time in Suez at the Red Sea. It was suggested that I ought to go with him on a trip to the East to learn more about drugs and medicine from other parts of the world. So here I am."

"I don't really have very much to do and the Raj pays my salary generously, so I could teach you in what is called Ayurveda. What do you think?"

"Yes, indeed."

"You could go on rounds with me if I have anyone in the house clinic," continued the Indian doctor.

The local doctor was an Indian Muslim named Hassan and he spoke also enough Arabic to communicate with Guillaume directly.

"Well, shall we start in the morning? It will certainly be good for me to have someone with whom I can share my thoughts on medicine. How long are you going to be here?"

"About six months, I think, until the ship is finished drying out, plastered, the barnacles taken off and loaded with merchandise and then we must wait for the right winds to take us to China."

"Six months is hardly enough time but perhaps you are a fast learner?"

"Yes, I think I can," said Guillaume.

Hassan began by giving Guillaume a list of plants and their cures or treatments. They must have gone through several hundred before Guillaume stopped Hassan.

"This one I don't think I'm familiar with."

Hassan began looking up on his shelves for something, which he didn't use very often.

"It's a climbing plant with elongated tubers and beautiful flowers and curved, wavy petals. It grows in greatest numbers in some coastal areas. Yes, here it is, and eh, would you like to have a few?"

"Oh, yes, please. What is it used for?"

"Well, these plump roots are used in skin, in the treatment of parasitic skin infections, internal worms and leprosy and are valuable in Ayurveda medicine."

"And it is only found in coastal areas around here, that is in India?"

"Yes, that's right."

"Could you send me some?" said Guillaume.

"Of course, I'd be happy to send you some."

"Including the preparation and a written document on which diseases it cures or treats and how often it does so?"

"That wouldn't be a problem."

"We have remedies for leprosy, parasitic skin infections, and so on, but this might be a better treatment."

"I would be glad to do it or you. By the way the lily's tuber-like rhizomes, the part which is underground, contain some ingredient for controlling gout and it has some anti-cancer properties as well."

"Fine, I look forward to writing you about so many things."

"The seeds are the least expensive and the flowers are most beautiful."

That afternoon they must have gone over hundreds of plants, looking for the best, and most effective. Occasionally, Guillaume would have one to trade, but unfortunately he didn't have a fresh one on hand and he would thus send it in the future by ship to Hassan.

"Are you familiar with what we Arabs call faufel? Some call it filfil they chew it all the time, and it is very good. I understand the Moors eat it every day, a green areca nut, it is a stupefying and intoxicant for any great pain they have." "Yes, I've heard of it,"

"Good then, we'll start again in the morning, if it's all right with you?"

"Of course, that'll be fine."

"Well, good night, Guillaume."

"Goodnight."

Guillaume went to his bedroom and stretched out after a hard trek through the brambles and grasses of the valley, which had tired him out and he easily fell asleep.

The following morning Guillaume met Hassan in the very large home of the Raj and together they went to the consulting room. There were two patients.

Hassan said to Guillaume: "Pick up this person's wrist and tell me by measuring his pulse what the man's condition is."

Guillaume did as he was told and held it for a minute's time thinking through all the symptoms the man had.

"I would like to see the man's urine as well."

"All right, and here you are," said Dr. Hassan handing Guillaume a glass of urine.

Guillaume looked at it, took a drop and placed it on the tip of his tongue.

"This man is suffering from an acute attack of appendicitis and from the look of his fever seems ready to have it out soon, yes, soon."

"That's right, but you should have noticed that from simply his pulse."

On the walls were mounted dozens of small bottles, which had fresh herbs and medicinal plant products in them. The man was wheeled into a smaller room-a surgery with its bottles of anesthetics on the wall. Guillaume spotted the name underneath the medicine and took some of them off the wall. He smelled the herbs and medicinal plants to assure him of their fresh potency and proceeded to grind them up into a sort of paste all the while being closely watched by Hassan.

"You might add a little lettuce and Syrian Rue and perhaps a little more opium to it. You see he is a pitta type: a man of medium build, sharp features. See his skin is warm, moist, pink with a little acne and his hair is fine, soft, and grey. Pitta types are having a tendency to bald, his forehead is medium with folds, and his eyes are red. And his lips are small, thin and dry, his nails are soft and pink and he has had regular, loose, often burning diarrhea. He enjoys a strong appetite. People of this type get irritable if their meals are milled," continued Hassan.

"All that from a patient?"

"All that and much more. You see, I've known the man for a long time and have thoroughly examined him. We can discover if the man's constitution leans towards vata, or wind, pitta or fire, or kapha, which stands for water, and all this will help us to know how an imbalance is likely to occur in them. Using the principle of like increases like, if we have a kapha water-dominant constitution then we may have a tendency to overweight, over-emotional nature, or eating too many sweets. So we should modify our diet and actions accordingly, and avoid sleeping in the daytime."

"You know him well as a patient?" inquired Guillaume.

"Yes, this practice and philosophy of Ayurveda is not only to restore balance and ease the pains and aches of the body, but also those of the spirit. Long before I got here and tried to practice Greek-Arab medicine I've been learning to keep a balance and to avoid extremes so that the existence of the Divine can be felt on the central nervous system," said Hassan. "Shall we proceed to the surgery?"

They went into another room and a nurse wheeled in the patient who had already been under anesthetics for about 15 minutes. Then Dr. Hassan began the surgery with Guillaume and the nurse assisting. When it was over the man was still under the anesthesia and would be for several more hours. Dr. Hassan prepared another pain reducing agent all formulated in a sponge, which he placed under the man's nose to keep him calm and to reduce his movements for a day or two until he began to heal properly. From surgery to his almost empty clinic they moved back and forth Guillaume keeping the doctor company and listening to what he said about Ayurveda.

"We try to cure the entire person not just the illness or disease, it is the same in Greek and Arabic medicine only the methods are somewhat different."

"I've been seeing that diagnosis is different and is much more difficult and yet the methods or treatments are much easier," said Guillaume, scrambling to keep up and write down as much as he could.

Still he was getting it through experience as he watched Dr. Hassan day by day go through his practice, sometimes with no patients at all, in which they would spend the entire day in discussions. Or showing Guillaume the preparations of herbal remedies for different diseases and different stages of a disease, whether it was on men or women, whether it was on a young child or an old man. All these things had to be taken into consideration and each of them modified the preparation. Guillaume was learning the intricate information.

By the time six months had passed, Guillaume was coming along very well and began to know Ayurveda, the Indian way of medicine. He began to think highly of this doctor and told him so. Hassan was very pleased to hear that. And he laughed.

"Actually, it is nothing what I do, Guillaume, I simply pass on the generosity of others to help other people through me. I will die some day with a fairly good conscience."

"Have you ever heard of ergot poisoning," asked Guillaume.

"No, don't believe I have, what is it?" said Hassan.

"You never heard of St. Anthony's Fire?"

"No, what is the cure for it?"

"There is no cure yet, I think."

"Ah, but what is it?"

"I think it is when the wheat stalk has turned black, and moldy, when the weather has misted, and the mist is blowing across the fields, and a lot of rain so that everything turns very humid."

"Yes, black and moldy, don't eat it, huh?"

"That's right, when the weather is wet, and the season is mild wheat stalks may turn somewhat black."

"I'll remember that, does it grow this far south, Guillaume?"

"No, I don't think so, I haven't seen wheat growing this far south."

"Well, you've warned me against a disease which I shall probably never see, but thank you, for telling me, we eat rice down here in the tropics as you know, and don't have that problem." said Hassan.

"Well, I guess, there is no problem here, not for that, I think you have problems with tropical illnesses, like bad air caused by dense clouds, people can get some fierce fevers for a while with it."

"Yes."

Guillaume was fairly careful with all the preparations and he wrote them all down.

There were many Arabs who had settled here who had not gone further than Kerala, who owned pepper plantations, and others were busily buying or planting their own plantations. Learning was made respectable. Islam had spread here up and down the coast and inward as well for fifty leagues, up to the mountains of the Western Ghats in the East.

Hassan asked Guillaume if he would like to go to the Ghats and take a look at the medicinal plants. And Guillaume said yes.

So, within a few weeks everything around the office had been taken care of, and they were ready to leave having borrowed a couple of horses from the Raj for the journey.

The following morning they began traveling an old dirt road, which led to the Ghats. The road followed a stream coming off the mountains, flowing with fresh water all the way westward to the sea. The stream narrowed the closer they got to the Western Ghats, and Guillaume could smell the humidity coming from them. For the last mile they walked the horses to bring them down gently from their hard ride. It was quite a long way for horses to canter in one day. But the exercise did the men some good as well. And when they got to the slopes of the Ghats the men let the horses feed on grass, they watered them, and tied them up, taking their saddles off, and brushed them off as well. They took out their tent put it up, and made a fire for the evening meal.

In the evening the men watched the stars, and saw many tiny bright flashes streaking across the sky. Looking at the River of Stars they saw them massed together like diamonds and pearls spilled on a darkened black surface.

"Allah has granted us a clear sky tonight," said Hassan.

"Filled with jewels."

"All we have to do is look around for He has given us everything we need and most of us with some of what we want in life."

"God is most generous with his giving, we could all learn from this if we only would."

"Frankly, I ought to get down on my hands and knees and thank the Almighty for having cured my patients. All I have done is make it possible for Allah to heal faster, that is all we physicians do is make it easier for people to heal."

"Yes," said Guillaume.

"May He be pleased with our observations, and now perhaps, we should get to bed for a full night's sleep, and get an early start tomorrow. We've a lot of ground to cover."

In the early morning's light the men got started feeding, and watering the horses

239

again, and eating a light breakfast of a couple of scrambled eggs.

They broke camp and began climbing up the slopes into the Ghats. After riding for some time the men finally got up to the 3.000 feet level, and completely out of breath they looked around and down from where they had come.

A cool breeze was rising up from below in a protected verdant canyon covered with montane forest and relaxed them. Looking down they could see a stream coming off a fall, and out of a jungle area into scrub forest.

Higher up they saw the wet evergreen forests they were looking for, and climbed up into the mist. Once in the forest the men opened their bags and Hassan showed Guillaume what he wanted to pick. He didn't want to pick the beautiful orchids for they had no medicinal value. Just looking at them seemed enough.

"Some day, Guillaume, all this will be cut down for the timber contained here. I know, it seems impossible, but men cannot see foresightedly, they just want what they can get right now, they rarely think ahead or for long. Worst of all is that they don't know restraint. They don't think of a forest but of timber. And they have not planted the same tree in that area."

"Do you think the Raj will allow that?" asked Guillaume.

"Well, he can't stop other kings who are larger than he is from doing it, you see, his kingdom is fairly small by most standards."

Suddenly, an explosion of birds careened out and upwards from where they had been startled. The trees suddenly became silent where before the chattering of the birds had almost been deafening.

"Oh, yes, there are also barking, and mouse deer, and the tiger which feeds on them, birds of every kind, plenty of macaques with tails like lions, giant squirrels, and, yes, I nearly forgot, the spotted deer as well. Sloth bear, too," said Hassan, who was by now short of breath.

He sat down and Guillaume joined him on the hillside in amongst the trees and the mist. At least it was cool, not hot like down on the plains where he could smell the horses when they sweat. After a relaxing pause they struggled upwards and onto the level ground where Hassan pointed out the various plants he wanted to collect: patchouli if it is well developed, lemon grass called the Sugandhi, which has a high level of quality and yield, the vetiver species, and the wild rose, which was in great demand.

"These make my aromatic plants, which I use in my practice, and they keep away the bugs, and smell sweet in my home," said Hassan.

They picked for a while moving down, and not gathering all in one area, and on down, the other side of the mountain. A little further ahead they came upon sweet basil in abundance, which was known to keep the mind rejuvenated, and strongly aromatic cinnamon. Finally their bags became filled and tied with a slender rope. Between them they had quite enough for one day. It would take them some time tomorrow to get all their bags down and into the waiting cart, which had come along after them. The man had gotten there sometime after they had gone to bed. They had also come upon some Sidhul and Guillaume watched as Hassan picked it out of the ground. The rhizomes of the plant would give an essential oil used to make perfumes and curry flavors, and keep the body resistant to diseases.

And a little further on down the mountain they came upon wild flowers, which they recognized and picked those known to have medicinal properties.

By now, the men had pretty much covered the area they wanted and began bringing down the bags, which they had brought with them. With the ropes tied behind them they shuffled the full bags.

A servant with the cart was busily making them something to eat. They were both bone tired after that trek, but in good spirits. The sun was beginning to set, and the heat of the day began to subside. Hassan and Guillaume looked forward to hot days, cool nights, especially the cool evenings where they could continue their conversations.

Pulling in their large bags the men put them into the cart next to the horses. Hassan petted them and spoke to them.

"Tomorrow, we'll go for the Indian Borage, the Vana Harida. We use the Borage to cure insect bites, headaches, fever, and bronchitis and the Vana as an ingredient in soap. Perhaps we'll find some Alpine Galanga, the roots are aromatic, it's a stimulant, and useful for diseases of the heart," said Hassan. "Perhaps we will find some sandalwood too, along with palm rose, and jasmine."

At that moment they all heard the cry of an elephant, and then it began to rain lightly. They found cover in the tent along with Asam the cart mover and fell asleep.

The following morning the men all got up early again, having worked out with Asam some of the tasks around the camp they were able to devote all their time to collecting spices.

Asam had breakfast ready for them in a flash. They ate and picked up their bags and walked up the mountainside's slopes until they found their spices and collected them.

In the afternoon they walked down to the stream they had seen the first day, and taking off their boots let their feet dip into the cold stream, instantly reviving their feet and themselves. Sitting by the stream for half an hour refreshed them. They put their boots back on and slowly moved toward home. Their bundles were bouncing a little up and down behind them on the ropes.

Finally getting home to their tent they saw Asam making dinner for them. The men threw their bundles in the cart and sat down to eat again. Then they watched the fire until quite late and discussed what they had found that day.

"Oh, I'm sure, other men are doing the same thing I'm doing, after all, there are other doctors up and down this coastal region, and so we are all using the forest's resources. We certainly don't damage the forests. There must be, well, at least a hundred doctors who do the same thing I do."

The last sunlight dipped and dappled the leaves with its golden hues moving ever so slowly toward the earth's darkness. The sounds of the forest died down for bringing everyone closer to slumber. The men were very tired and unable to hold their heads up anymore, so Asam carried the conversation until he found he was talking to himself.

The next day was their last, and they simply walked around for the fun of it. Upward they went, up to the 7.000 feet level where the cold blew against their skin, reddening it. The men enjoyed the cold on their bodies after a summer of hot sun and the humidity, which went along with it.

Then they started running down the slopes as if they were kids, to keep their feet going for if in an instant they slipped they would both have fallen, and possibly broken an arm or a leg or perhaps even broken their stride, fallen and killed themselves. They were laughing recklessly as they went; yet their mature bodies were out of shape, but still they continued running on and on and on until they were both finally exhausted.

Asam saw them on the mountain when they came into view and thought that they were having trouble. But no, they didn't. They were having fun. He thought the men were crazy to run that way down the mountain. Now and then he saw them leaping and jumping over obstacles with almost complete abandon.

After Hassan and Guillaume had gotten back they looked completely exhausted. Asam had some water waiting for them, which they drank in huge gulps and threw on one another, laughing all the while. Finally, they fell on the grass, and in a moment's time they were fast asleep.

After an hour Asam started another cooking fire, and prepared them another meal. He woke them up, and served them the food. They thanked Asam, and after eating they lied down and instantly fell asleep again.

The next morning they returned riding home to the land of the Raj.

Sometime in November it was time to depart again. The pilot came for Guillaume. The winds were right for them blowing eastward. Their ship, with its upswept sterns, looked like new with fresh sails, and the sides of the SeaWolf also seemed brand new. Everything had been swabbed down with vegetable oil on the inside of the ship and outside, lime was applied below the waterline to kill or repel the shipworms and fish oil smeared on the hull as a preservative. The SeaWolf was ready.

Gayatri strolled by one afternoon, and they looked at one another for long moments. She smiled.

The following day the final preparations were being made to get the supplies of pepper on board when the last thing was placed on the ship. The other ships had been provisioned before the larger one, and had also been reconditioned.

The men were anxious to go having had little to do during all these months.

As the ship was sliding backward being pushed by some of the Raj's men, Guillaume waved and whispered her name, Gayatri. Slowly the ship moved, and then caught the puffs of air in her white new sails. And then with ever increasing speed, the

SeaWolf started sailing faster until the wind caught the sails to their fullest extent, like huge breasts, Guillaume thought.

Changing landscapes constantly flowed by. And with the wind continuing to push them along they came to the tip of the subcontinent, and as the ship reached the open ocean leaving India behind.

In the morning they still saw new land but it was different, for Sirandib came into view. Still they kept sailing, as they were interested in the far side of the island, Adam's Peak. This they reached in the early evening, and where they were they could see lights going up the mountain. Pilgrims were climbing the old worn dirt trail with their lanterns all the way to the summit.

According to legend Adam's Peak was supposed to be the first footprint of the first man.

From the ship it looked like tiny fireflies were going to their home in the sky. The ship docked at a place called Abrir on the southern side of Sirandib, the Island of Rubies. These roughened jewels they bought there were uncut and unpolished, but Solomon had a polisher on board whom he set immediately to work on the gems with his wooden handled diamond polisher in his cabin. This man could carve anything, and carve it exceptionally well.

Every year Solomon's cargo changed, some years it was the horns of the rhinoceros, and plenty of gold, timber as in poon, and teak for ship's masts or fine furniture, another year might be muslins, and jewels, and medicinals. Every year was different. And every year Solomon went round, and made a survey of what people desired here, and did they have the money to pay? And in India what did they have to sell, some things remained the same cargo such as pepper, cardamom, and cinnamon, and kampher. Solomon's powers of observation were legendary, and quite beyond normal. He measured men in his mind, and didn't speak down to them, but on an equal basis, respecting what they had to say no matter how dumb, and ignorant it sounded. He would simply make a counter argument, which was logical, and right, and destroyed the other men's argument without hurting their feelings.

The pilot was the same way with those men whom he knew to be quite ignorant of reading, and calligraphy. All of which made him greater in other men's eyes. He always tried to make them think for themselves rather than simply say that something was or was not so without giving them an explanation. It took a little bit of extra time, but by doing so the men in the end nearly worshiped him.

If Solomon had any faults or vices it was that he was too indulgent with his men. He always treated them well. By taking the initiative he was a leader of men who also looked out for them, but who also had the panache of a younger man.   Thus was Solomon, the pilot navigator.

It would take them another month to reach the Straits of Selahit if they were lucky. But they kept nearly the same latitude as they passed Lamuri Island, they knew they were about to pass the huge northern tip of Al-Ramni Island, passing its top, straight into the sea of Harkand and its islands before the town, and Kalah-Bar settlement on the Hanhang peninsula.

In this small town full of Arabs and Persians with their gardens and high walls they rested for several days. When they got enough water to continue they waved goodbye and sailed in a southerly direction.

From Kalah Bar they passed the sea of Salahit. Everyone was tense. For here they had to watch out for pirates, they could be anywhere, and knowing this area they weren't surprised to be a possible victim of a small fleet of pirate ships coming around the corner of the Pahang peninsula. But the Arabs were ahead of them, waiting, with their Greek fire lit, and ready. And the others with their accurate crossbows and training with them also waited for the pirates. They stayed away from the small islands, which they feared could hide fleets of ships, and kept to the main channel. Still there were just too many emerald-green islands; some of them were elongated, others were short, some tall and small, others wide and flat with palms, and jagged pines protruding out to sea. After a while they began to imagine pirate ships around every island, but they saw nothing. And then they suddenly saw them and began to tremble.

The pirate ships came closer, perfectly confident that the three vessels were under-armed. A few spears were thrown from the largest pirate ship. Most of the men were under the railing and could not be seen.

Solomon disappeared into his cabin shattering Guillaume's composure. When the pirate ship came within twenty yards the Arabs turned up the handle on their Greek Fire weapon, and sent the burning jelly flying into space to hit the vessel in its sails. Then followed by another blast at the surprised pirates who simply stood around looking at the fiery display as if they were stupefied.

All of a sudden the fifteen men who had been hiding stood up and started firing their crossbows, several missed, but many others found their marks, men fell over and died. The pirate ship caught fire soon enough, and began wobbling around steering in circles, and as it came around again another burst of Greek Fire hit the remaining men who hadn't jumped into the sea, and caught them. It was a gristly sight. Men were burning, and jumping off their ship into the sea.

Guillaume hoped he'd never see this sight again. The burning men were screaming pathetically. Yet they kept on, and the other ships backed off not wanting to have anything to do with the SeaWolf. In a little time the remaining pirate ships had disappeared, sailing back to the overgrown jungled islands.

After a while, the Arabs put out the lit flame-thrower. And everybody was shouting, dancing, and laughing so much the first mate bowled over, and the ship lost its bearing, and began to swing around, but

Guillaume caught it in time to turn it into its correct path.

By that time the pilot came out of his cabin, and said, "Well, we haven't lost the crew, and ship to enemy fire. How many men did we lose?"

"None."

"And how many did the enemy lose?"

"Well, one of their major ships is, as you can see, on fire, and burning, and they lost about twenty men, I think, the rest of their ships, and crews have gone back in hiding and lost their confidence, and now that they know that cargo ships have Greek Fire, I think they'll hesitate before coming back. But if they do they'll come perhaps with a smaller ship, and fewer men, next time."

"Not bad," said the pilot, "you've done well, and I see that you've got your timing down, you know when to let them have it, hah-hah-hah!"

They were sailing toward one of the smaller islands as the channel widened.

"The island on your left is called Singapura, and the one on your right is named Bintan, the other one is called Bantan. The ones in the back of us are

Sinki, and the big island, back there, is the Sri Vijaya kingdom," said the first mate.

The first mate slowly turned the rudder to the right, and the huge ship began turning toward the left. He began turning the ship parallel to the coast on their left, yet far enough away from the breakers. The men had turned the heavy white lanteen sail toward the wind let it fill out, and the ship cutting the water gained speed.

"The island coming up is named Tiyuma, we'll see it in a while. Yes, there it is, but it's a long way off still. We'll stop there and get our water from a beautiful waterfall, and perhaps sleep on the beach and watch the lizards fight. There really isn't much to do."

They already had water on board, but it wasn't fresh. In the afternoon they sailed to Tiyuma, and a number of the men hauled the skiff to the ship, loaded it with water kegs, and sailed to the beach to get them filled with fresh water. The men proceeded to a small waterfall spilling over groups of rocks, and down into the ocean. Here they filled the kegs and brought them back.

It was beginning to darken, and the men gathered firewood building a large fire on the beach to show the men in the ship that they were all right. The next day with their water kegs on board they sailed on eastward for the large island of Ray.

They saw the jungles of Ray fairly close, but couldn't make out any people or signs of life. After many days of sailing north they reached the way station of Kora Baru, which the Arabs there called Brunai.

The men docked the ship, and the pilot began talking to a few men who welcomed them there. These men had already cut the kampher trees letting the tree's sap of kampher come out. And they had gotten plenty of gaharu wood. The small amounts of gold and diamonds were also welcome by Solomon.

The medicinal use of kampher crystals was well known as a stimulant to the heart and blood vessels, but also for incense and ointments.

The Arabs who lived there would go into the montane forests, and talk to the Dahyak people into cutting down special aloe-wood timber for them for a small fee, and negotiating for the rest of the articles. The pilot's men then got a chance to stay and rest on the land cultivated by the Arabs, while they unloaded the ship again.

Solomon took a sailor aside who knew Guillaume well, and cautioned him to keep an eye out for Guillaume for the pilot knew that Guillaume often had his head in the clouds, and would simply walk off into the jungle without anyone with him, and that this would endanger him if he were alone. The large man nodded, smiling.

Then having unloaded everything they began packing everything back loading the kampher trees on top of the teak. In less than four days the men were ready to sail to the coast of Cochin Chyna in the land of Champa, to a place in a Muslim port called Sanf Fulaw. The way over took them twenty-five days and was uneventful, simply blue sky, and various shades of indigo-blue water.

At Sanf Fulaw the pilot found his Vermilion bird, something he'd been waiting for for a long time. He thanked the man for getting it, keeping it alive, and in good health, and paid the Arab in gold for it. Three years before Solomon had negotiated with the man for the bird, so well known in China, but seldom seen as it came from the interior of this area and this area only. The man thanked him and wished him a good journey.

Then they sailed for the Gates of China; a number of rocks projecting up from the ocean, which must at all cost be avoided for out in the middle of the ocean there was no land anywhere nearby where one could land.

Having passed this point they had another three weeks to sail for Khanfu, indicating that the final destination of the journey was soon staring them in the face.

The next morning they had a squall. But by mid-morning it had turned into a tufan, the Arabic word for typhoon. Rather than lose their mast, the men quickly furled the sails, and made fast the main spar, while the ship's rudder did not make much difference in their direction to Khanfu. The pilot was shouting orders left and right. They were falling, rolling, rising, and churning as if they were on bucking horses. Everything was wet and beginning to tear. And they began to wonder if they would ever get to the Pearl River. They thought they had seen the coast of China.

CHINA

A few sweltering days later they again sighted the coast of As-Sin, and this time the port of Kan P'hu as the Chinese called it, or Khanfu, as the Arabs had named it, in the province of Kuang-Nan Tung. At last they saw the tip of Dawanshan, the minaret of a mosque, the Kwang Ta at the mouth of the Pearl River known to the Arabs as the "Great River".

It served as the only point to mark the harbor and as a lighthouse and had been built by Arabs a few centuries ago. Then the Mosque of Remembrance came into view and this happy sight instantly washed away their recent troubles.

The SeaWolf stopped at Ju-Chóu or T' un-mên island, commonly referred to as Pei-tu. A small fast boat rowed up alongside, filled with a number of large rough-looking men. Their leader said something to them in a language they didn't understand, so they said something back to him in Arabic, greeting him politely.

The man understood and replied in a flawless and perfect Arabic.

"You need to follow me now."

And so they followed his boat up into the harbor's mouth about a quarter of a league from land, dropped anchors, and furled their sails among old and new junks.

Another much larger boat rowed up and some Chinese began to lash their boat to the ship. After that, the officer in charge instructed the pilot that he had the authority to inspect and take off all the cargo: ambergris, soft gold brocades, ivory, rhinoceros horns, cloves, frankincense, foreign satins, and especially huge bundles of pepper, timber, and a very small bag of pearls or jewels.

Everything was to be put in storage for up to six or more months or until the last foreign ship arrived. The Government had first choice too of what it wanted for duty taxes and then they would be allowed to sell the rest of their cargo in the markets taking their profit. All this Solomon already knew, having been here before. He said "yes" to everything the Chinese demanded to put them at ease.

And after an hour the Chinese seemed to be satisfied. They gave Solomon a piece of paper, detailing the amount and numbers of goods in Arabic and Chinese and they left after taking the entire cargo with them.

What Solomon and his sailors wanted of course was Celadon, elegant Celadon, pale greenish-blue like light moss Celadon. Celadon like jade, Celedon to make your mouth water, and off-white glazed bowls that glowed with the light through which one could see the shadows of his fingers and hands, almost translucent, and made in this dynasty of the Northern Sung.

That night the Persian captain and Solomon had a long talk in the pilot's cabin and in the middle of it in the dark of night an explosion ripped the silence around them, and then another, and another. Rockets were going off into the sky and at first they just stood there taking it all in and everyone thought it was some kind of celebration with the city so lit up momentarily against the dark night's sky.

A few minutes later they saw multitudes of people scattering this way and that and they knew something was wrong, terribly wrong. And then they saw it, a huge white explosion throwing tiny rockets here and there in the air, rocking their ship and all the other ships in the harbor. The force literally rocked every boat and ship by making large waves and sinking a few of the smaller ones. It illuminated the towering spire of the Light Tower minaret of Huaisheng Mosque.

Shouts of "Ya Allah!" went around the ship and the pilot came running, asking for the physician.

Guillaume went over to Solomon.

"Yes, pilot."

"Can you swim?" asked Solomon in a hurry.

"Of course not, I'm a monk."

"What does your being a monk have to do with it? Well, I can show you how to swim if you've got the guts, dog fashion, here take these gems and start swallowing them and be quick about it!"

"Swallowing them?" repeated Guillaume.

"Yes!" said Solomon, "swallow them all, right now, dammit, before we lose our chance!"

Guillaume began swallowing the pearls and rubies three or four at a time as quickly as he could. The pilot was also swallowing diamonds and another man nearby, Abu Bakr, was swallowing emeralds. After they had swallowed all the gems Solomon began taking off his clothes and instructed the men to do the same. They all folded their clothes into small bundles and wrapped them in waterproof canvas. Then they tied hemp rope around the bundles and themselves, and placed some wide-brimmed Chinese hats on their heads. Once more they looked at the scene with all the blowing and burning of the town, bright lit against a dark night's sky.

"Boom! Boom! Boom!"

Huge black and white clouds formed a background for the rockets. Now and then another explosion lit up the landscape. The pilot took them to the back of the ship and went over the side on an anchor rope tied to a deck rail. He slowly stepped into the water, followed by Guillaume and the other men who had swallowed the gems. Now all of them were in the river and watching Solomon.

"Follow what I am doing and just do what I do and nothing else," he said.

"Boom! Boom! Boom!"

And it seemed as though the whole southeastern side of the river town was blowing up and burning with pieces of wood flying through the air. No one noticed the three men dog paddling and others swimming like a fish, all going slowly up the broad estuary of the Great River. Finally they reached shore near some trees and bushes to hide themselves in, and they unwrapped their bundles. They were shivering badly and put their clothes on.

No one could see them for long in the rush of people trying to get out of the way of the burning quarter of town. People were escaping in panic.

"Boom! Boom! Boom! Boom!"

Houses were catching fire. The burning and explosions kept getting worse and one could smell the stench of burning flesh and acrid smoke of the fire. Nobody noticed the men running one after the other in bare feet. People were intent on saving themselves and took little notice of the four fugitives who kept their heads lowered and partly covered by the big hats.

They got out of the city and passed the multitudes of people and slowed down to a walking speed again.

Finally the pilot meandered to a very large house up on a hill, away from the burning city. They went up to the front of the house and knocked on the door. Someone came running to let them in.

A fat old Chinese man received them. He knew Solomon well and spoke almost perfect Arabic. He laughed a lot and moved his long black pigtail back and forth.

"It's about time you got here, what a wonderful opportunity to see our river city on fire, that's perfect, and you all look most Chinese, I might add."

"Yes, well, we didn't waste much time," Solomon said, rubbing his belly.

"I think I'm going to have to require you all take and accept the hospitality of our home for several days," said Li Chung, the old Chinese, ruefully.

"Oh, thank you my good sir, I am sure we can arrange that, at least until we've passed the gems into your hands," laughed Solomon out loud with a twinkle in his eye.

Li Chung laughed at the deception and took them to the side of the house reserved for guests, and presented them with fitting clothes. Then he sat them down for a meal of rice his servants had just cooked. Li Chung asked them questions about their long journey. He hadn't seen the pilot for a couple of years and wanted to know all about his adventures.

It turned out the Chinese authorities were taxing people to death in the last few years, and everyone had taken to smuggling.

It was a unique way of doing something about it: swallowing gems and pretending to visit someone in the wealthy section of the city, and under the pretense of a huge city fire! But every captain had been hit hard in his profits, and had taken to smuggling so the profit margins were rapidly thinning.

The next evening an unusually beautiful Chinese girl of seventeen in a beautiful light yellow silk dress was invited and came to the house to tell the guests a story about a monkey who could speak, and who could travel through realms of being on his way to the West. This story seemed so odd and bizarre that Guillaume was astonished and intensely drawn in listening to it. And he made sure that his attention was well focused so that he could relate the story to anyone else in the future.

In a few days time they all defecated into a small finely screened wooden box over a toilet. A young Chinese boy came in bowed, and removed the screened box.

Li Chung was very happy he didn't have to pay the authorities the duty tax on every consignment and neither did the pilot nor the Persian captain.

In an office of a rather large building a few leagues away near the beach sat a man in a black silk dress. He was an official, wearing a small black hat with red buttons on top over a pigtail. His double-position was being the superintendent of merchant shipping at Khanfu and the inspector of maritime trade. In the rapidly decreasing foreign intercourse of trade the government wished a larger portion of the profits from trade, so he began thinking how to do this without upsetting the Arabs, knowing quite well that 200 years before, they had become enraged, sacking and burning the city and taking their profits with them, for being too heavily taxed.

He kept thinking how he could gain for the empire 30% of everything taken from the Arabs. Profits were going down, but there were as many ships in the harbor as always. Yet the profits were plunging. The superintendent put soldiers on board of all the vessels in order to keep watch over every man on the ships. Still he couldn't keep the stolen profits from sliding and he didn't know why.

Suddenly, the left-portion of the city exploded and people were running for their lives. Pieces of wood, material and bodies were flying through the air. The explosions rocked the buildings, and blew a hole in his window and for a few minutes the superintendent was helplessly hiding behind his desk.

The explosions continued for half an hour. Finally the superintendent stood up and sat down in his chair for he knew beyond a shadow of a doubt that pilots were either taking advantage of the situation or more likely started the conflagration to get some of their goods to shore. The superintendent had a knife. With it he kept stabbing his papers. He was a very angry man. And at one point in the stabbing of papers and another moment of anger he put the short thin knife with a fancy blade right through his hand.

The pilot got a note, which could be redeemed for money in Baghdad at Li Chung's trading office. Solomon was happy, Chung was delighted and Guillaume very pleased, knowing he had done this man a good deed and had helped get the ship, its crew and himself a bit further along the way. The note was folded in such a way so that it could be fitted into the pilot's enormous dark emerald–green ring with a silver Jewish Star of David on it.

Three nights later they all swam back to the ship and slept like tired children. The soldiers on board having watched the terrible fire, were still discussing it, they hadn't noticed a thing regarding the excursion of Solomon and his men, who climbed back on the ship quietly and unnoticed and went straight to their cabins.

The following morning Solomon called his men and took them into his cabin. There he gave Abu Bakr a small ruby and gave the other man an emerald. And Guillaume received half a dozen large, natural pearls. It was a great reward for little work. He then told them not to mention a word of their adventure and their profit to anyone. Solomon then told Abu Bakr and the other men to take their gems and put them in a safe place and the men left.

Then the pilot was holding back Guillaume and explained to him, that in case of emergency he wanted Guillaume to take over. If something happened to him or the Persian captain. And Guillaume promised he would do it.

"Good," said Solomon, "it may even be that the captain is also killed or badly injured and then you will take over if you're still here and you've got a crew to sail the ship and you need to learn how to navigate this it."

"I understand," said Guillaume.

269

Late that evening they all sat around having nothing to do and watched the stars. The stink from the city was overpowering.

The following day was like many of the other days on board, filled with repairing the sails, the poon tree mast had held up well in the squalls and hadn't snapped. They did not have to get the teak masts out, and most of the tackle was also intact.

Guillaume had no idea just how far he would go to the East and Southeast, or what adventures lay in store for him. Solomon kept him busy with learning the kamal. This was a rectangular shaped piece of wood with a string going through the middle attached to it and knots in the string for different places and to find the latitude at sunset. It was almost as efficient as his more complicated astrolabe.

The ropes had to be oiled again with vegetable oil to preserve them now that the cargo had been taken. The ship had thousands of hand-drilled holes through which hundreds of leagues of coir rope made of coconut cords were passed through, holding the vessel together. The flexibility of the ship made for a real rough going, but the ship stayed together without a nail in it. On the outside of the ship the holes were smeared with a mixture of tree gum and lime and on the inside the holes were plugged up with coconut husk.

The canvas sails had to be taken to the beach and unfurled completely. Some of the ship's crewmembers were known as sewers and they were instantly looking for tares. Within a week the job of stitching the sails was nearly finished.

The ship was also beached with her carved and galleried stern to the sea, and the hull needed to be scrubbed and smeared with oil made from the fat of fish, or coarse lime, and camel-tallow if it could be had. All this was necessary to keep the barnacles and worms at a minimum from eating holes in the ship. Their very large ocean-going vessel looked grand, all nearly 200 feet of her once she had been completely refurbished.

In the evenings nearly always Abu Bakr would relate his yarns to them. He told us of a certain captain named 'Abharah from Kirman who eventually became a captain of a China ship. And he knew the sea very well for he never had an accident on a voyage, which was a wonder. He had never heard of a man who had sailed the sea to China without some mishap and returned unharmed.

Guillaume was becoming restless and the next day he asked Solomon if he could go ashore.

"Certainly, but you'll need some Chinese paper money. Here take this," and he gave some banknotes to Guillaume.

Guillaume kept turning the paper money over and over in his hand and looked at it.

Guillaume was advised by Solomon to take a crewman along to go ashore.

And shortly a crewman was rowing across the distance between the ship and shore.

"What's your name?" asked Guillaume to broke the uncomfortable silence between them.

"Hatim," replied the man.

When they got to the shore, they stored the boat with a willing local Chinese man whose job it was to watch people's boats and whom they paid. Then Guillaume and Hatim headed towards that part of town, which hadn't burned down.

They came upon a businessman with a small bamboo shop cooking rice. Sitting down Hatim said something to the cook in Chinese and he served them some hot soup with prawns in it. Guillaume had to be told how to eat prawns, as he'd never had them before. And in his bowl underneath some of the rice Guillaume found a tiny baby squid. Hatim laughed at him. And then they both ended up laughing.

The air was still thick with dark dirty-grey smoke clouds. Guillaume bought Hatim's soup, they got up and wandered around town and finally out into the wasteland of the city where flowers grew along the side of roads and plants grew vigorously in the tilled land. Guillaume smelled the odor of the deep black soil. It smelled good.

Local travelers went by in their hired hand-carried sedan chairs with ladies who stuck out their heads struggling with large white circular flopping hats holding them down with their hands. They looked, stared and gawked at the foreign visitors as their palanquins went on down the road.

Guillaume laughed, and so did Hatim. Guillaume became more comfortable with the sculpted landscape he was seeing. At first all the mountains seemed strange until he fixed his eyes on them and realized that all the trees had been cut down and the mountains shaped by the weather and rains and there was nothing to hold the soil together and so the mountains were sculpted by landslides in strange and beautiful ways.

Toward the late afternoon Guillaume turned around and he and Hatim returned to the ship. Hakim wanted to stop at the food shop again, and Guillaume consented. They sat down and ordered green tea, which Guillaume had never had.

Twilight was coming down on the city, people were beginning to hang lanterns outside their doors and the scenario took on a natural look with the wind gently blowing some of the stink away.

Suddenly Guillaume saw something he recognized: a Mozarabic hat in the crowd, taller than the Chinese and Guillaume strained to see, and then he thought he saw Rabi.

Rabi? He thought. It couldn't be. But indeed it was he, and he did not recognize Guillaume, even though he came his way.

"Rabi!" shouted Guillaume, "Racemundo is that you?"

First Guillaume called him by his Gothic-Latin name and then by his Arabic name: Rabi ibn Zayd.

"Yes, it's me. Is it you, Guillaume? Oh, yes, it is, and what for God's sake are you doing here?" Rabi said with an incredulous look on his face.

Guillaume told him his long story and he was talking so fast that Rabi had to slow him down.

"And how long are you going to be here, Rabi?" asked Guillaume.

"Well, I've been here for several months on business for the Caliph looking for porcelain and doing a bit of business here for myself as well.

Guillaume laughed.

"I'm glad I found you!"

"And how long have you been here?" inquired Rabi and grinned.

"Oh, just a week, maybe a little less," answered Guillaume.

"And not doing much I gather? Well, tomorrow you'll have to meet a man I'd like to introduce you to if you come to the office of pharmaceutics, around 9 in the morning?"

"Alright," said Guillaume, "but where is the office?"

"Oh, it's that large building over there. I'll surely be able to introduce you to him and he might be able to make some official arrangements for you as a courtesy to me, however, I don't promise anything," said Rabi.

That evening Guillaume went to the pilot and asked him how long they would be there and where they might be going next? And Solomon told him that they would be there for about four or five months and then they would go up to the capital, then on to Khanju and Qansu, and finally they would sail up to Al-Sila and the island of Waqwaq. Then they'd sail back here to Khanfu. It should take about a year or more because of the typhoon season when we'd have to lay up.

"After that we'll probably sail south to the land of Al-Zabag on the island of Juva, also called Swarra Dwipa or the island of gold and from there we go south southeast into unknown waters."

"Alright, then, may I have your permission to stay here and wait for you to come back?" asked Guillaume.

"Of course you can, physician, although I'll be missing your services," he said gloomily.   "And you'll have to find me a replacement, a good one, like you."

Guillaume was very pleased and excited.

The following day he arrived promptly on time at the entrance to the enormous office building and was met there by Rabi.

"Come with me."

A few minutes later Rabi and Guillaume walked into Lu To-hsun's tiny office and Rabi made introductions all round.

"He was first in the examinations for this office two years ago and he has also revised the Classic of Pharmaceutics," said Rabi proudly as if he had a hand in it.

"Ah," said Guillaume, "very nice."

"I think Lu will be glad to help you find out about the medicinal plants you are looking for, and what's more, he may be able to help you in studying with him if you are going to be here for say another five months or longer, and perhaps he can help make arrangements for you to study Chinese medicine."

"That would be fantastic!" said Guillaume.

Then he realized that they would know back home that he was alive in China when Rabi looked up Al-Hakam and Jacques.

"Alright! I'll send round my interpreter and you and he can make arrangements with Lu."

Guillaume was ecstatic. The following day he and the interpreter Wang Chou, who could speak fluent Arabic and Lu the Chinese official, who spoke a little Arabic sat down and began planning the best and fastest ways to do their jobs. The interpreter, Wang could only give them four hours a day and both Lu and Guillaume thought that would serve them well.

He bought a small house in town after selling the pearls Solomon gave him and he managed to set aside enough money to purchase enough food and survive for as long as a year.

Then he inquired to find a replacement doctor who might want to sail with Solomon on the ship. He found a Chinese doctor who was willing to sail north. He could speak Arabic. Guillaume asked the doctor to make detailed notes of medicinal plants he encountered from Korean and Japanese doctors he met, and to learn something about their theories and principles of medicine.

"I will do that, I had wanted to do something like that in any case," said the Chinese doctor.

He promised the pilot that he would take good care of his crew.

The next day Guillaume went with Wang Chou to the government building to see Lu, and Guillaume's training in Chinese medicine began.

As the mutual interest between Lu, Wang Chou, and Guillaume began to grow the tale of what they were doing started to spread, and a few others became interested as well. A Chinese doctor stopped by and stayed. His name was Chuang Tzu and now and then he would say something to the other three. They began comparing the medicines, medical practices, theories, similarities and differences as well as the underlying principles between them in humeral theory in the medicine of China, India and Arabia.

Eventually, Lu went to the Records Office to see if he could find out whether other foreigners at other times had made such inquires, and found one note which said that an Arabian doctor had come to China, and bought up a large quantity of Ginseng in the ninth century. No name, no date. And this was all that was written about it.

Their work and exchange of medical information went on well into the autumn, and now and then Guillaume would put in ten hours of work, coming back to his little two room cottage he passed the white naphtha filled lanterns in the evening swinging as they did with a breeze, and the leaves of trees came blowing down with people quickly hurrying home.

He thought that the Chinese and the Arabs had the same principles and theories of the humeral system of medicine. All that was different was the process, there were differences in the techniques of treatment; acupuncture, for example, was unknown in the West and this interested Guillaume. However, they both relied on plant medicine, but with different uses for it. Yet they were getting some of the same results. And the more he heard about the Middle Kingdom the more he was itching to go to Zhong-guo.

The following day Lu gave Guillaume another good drug called gan cao, Licorice root, which he said helped with tuberculosis and ulcers as well. In almost all cases the powdered herb was most effective. And Guillaume gave Lu a recipe for neem and turmeric from India used to heal chronic ulcers, and scabies.

And with each drug he showed them how it was administered. He also in the light of their own experiments and observations, described the general and special botanical characters of the plants in great detail, as well as indicating their habitats and what was best selected from each and how each stem, leaf, root and seeds were used. What time of day: morning, afternoon, or evening to pick them. There were many drugs, and diseases discussed by the men.

Within a period of about five months they were finished with the first draft of comparison between Greek, Arabic, Indian and Chinese medicine. Guillaume had learned that the Chinese were able to cure smallpox by injecting the arm with a small amount of the disease of a healthy patient, which then makes the body somehow so resistant to the disease that it cannot come down with it.

This was one of the most interesting things Guillaume ever learned there. He thought about it for a week and then asked the Chinese physician to vaccinate him and show him the way to do it.

That afternoon Guillaume felt the need to pray at the Huaisheng Mosque and walked over looking up at the tall minaret before going in to the prayer hall of the Mosque to take off his shoes. He knelt down on a prayer mat and gave thanks to God for his having made it safely across the oceans and for everything else. He felt grateful for the way his life had turned out.

A few minutes later a trio of Arabs walked up to Guillaume and one said in Arabic: "Aren't you in the wrong church, Christian?"

Guillaume had redressed himself in his black Benedictine robes.

"This is a house of the Lord of Lords, Master of the worlds, is it not? I can pray here as everyone who prays here to the Ultimate Master of the Universe," said Guillaume standing up.

The Arabs shrugged, and walked away into another room of the Mosque.

Guillaume said: "Perhaps, I ought to go and also try praying in the Jewish temple here on the other side of town."

The superintendent offered a reward to the first of his sergeants and his men if they could find out how and where the profits were going ashore. His hand was killing him, but the wound was healing, yet he felt like a fool when he had to tell his superior what happened. All the Chinese on shore had been replaced by his men, his best men; small businessmen, people who lived nearby, cooks, restaurant owners, people strolling by or sitting, and drinking green tea, some walking with their paper umbrellas, those pulling carts or large wagons. Everyone in that part of town had been replaced, had saturated the area with his spies. And they all behaved quite naturally, some were walking around, others were engaged in group-discussions. There were some men crossing a wooden bridge. It looked as though everything was proper.

Guillaume felt edgy coming home late at night with people staring at him. He thought this was new. They hadn't done that before. But no one stopped him or even came up to him.

The superintendent simply found no relief in his frustration. He grit his teeth at night. He tossed and turned, couldn't keep his eyes shut, and he got up and drank a glass of water. Then he practically fell into bed, but couldn't sleep. But when he finally did fall asleep he automatically began gritting his teeth. This happened over and over all night long.

"Oh, Master," said his one and only attendant in the morning, "may I fix your bandage?"

"You may," said the tall man in an unpleasant voice, "and you may also bring some rope, so that you may bind my arm to my waist. And bring me a hot pot of tea!"

He hadn't promised that he wouldn't shout, he told himself as he gripped the edge of the chair feeling utterly helpless, a victim of his own mastery.

"Yes Master," said the attendant.

"I am going to have a wonderful day today, and I am going to catch those damned crooks, who do they think they are kidding, by hiding all that profit from my hands?"

With his teacup in his hand he stepped outside, then back into his office. He closed

284

the door, put his cup on the desk, sat down and wept.

Guillaume walked around to places he'd never gone before on his free days and decided to go up river.

Two boats were placed in the river with timbers on them and two A-frames were used to raise the bridge frames and the middle was moved into place over the initial frames, then it was connected with bamboo lashing and they wove a four-sided arch into position with the A-frames removed.

Guillaume wondered where the water came from, was it from a mountain? He did not know that canals were being dug all over China at that time, so that people with goods could go to places directly and not have to go the long way around saving time.

Guillaume went back to the ship to visit Solomon and told him about his desire to go for some time into the country's interior to explore things. Solomon strongly suggested that Guillaume ought to take with him someone who spoke Chinese and Arabic well enough to be able to communicate. He also invited Guillaume to go along to the house of the gem merchant the following evening. And Guillaume jumped at the opportunity.

The Superintendent had lost the battle. How would he please Emperor Zhao Kuangy? Would he now too have to kowtow to the Emperor of the Northern Sung. How could he now curry favor with him? Would he be a prisoner all his life? What kind of a life was that?

The following night they let down the dingy, the crewmen rowed them to shore and Guillaume and Solomon made their way to the house of Li Chung. The houseboy let them in and then came Li Chung to greet them.

"So, you've come to pay me a friendly visit and not a business one, eh?" said the Chinese man, "good!"

"Yes, we're here simply to say hello, and tell you that our ship is ready to go, and the weather is coming along, so it's nearly time for us to leave," said Solomon.

"And I see Guillaume was interested in coming here with us, interested in the pretty girl we had here last time, I suppose?" said Li Chung.

"No, not really, but I was interested if she knew more stories and poetry," Guillaume exclaimed.

"Well, whatever, we shall have a feast, and I will send a boy for her," said the gem merchant.

Their meal was delicious. Duck was served with many side dishes. After dinner when the talking became lighter a knock on the door was heard, and a servant went to answer it. The beautiful Chinese girl in an outstanding red silk dress who had previously told the story about the monkey king came in. This time the girl sang poetry for them while playing a Chinese string instrument.

"That was charming wasn't it?" inquired Li Chung.

"Delightful, radiant, yes," exclaimed Solomon, trying to be very polite.

"I thought it was pretty, and sonorous," added Guillaume.

The Chinese girl sensed their approval and thanked them. She stood up, bowed, and got ready to leave, carefully packing her lute over her shoulder.

Guillaume asked her name.

"I'm Quin Lee," said the girl wondering what Guillaume wanted more of her than she had already given.

By now the servants had put up the scrolled paintings by fixing them to wooden handles. Various gentlemen began to arrive for the viewing. And Guillaume was invited to see this, thinking how Jacques would have loved to see all this.

Later Li Chung went with them into an extremely large back yard and told them: "If you want to have your work done easily, you must work very hard. There is no getting away from it. But hard work is not nearly enough. As in calligraphy and writing, painting is the same, one may have no idea at all how a master gets simplicity, ordinariness into his work, but it takes much more sweat. Many people have high intelligence, but no talent or creativity. Can you let your mind fly? If so, you know what I mean. And if you know what I mean then you have 'it'. You may have 'it' and not know it, your school may not know it, and your parents may not know it. But 'it' knows. You see, in the daytime I am an Art dealer, but at night I'm a gem merchant," said Li chuckling. "Suppose, for example, you are 'lost' and don't know what or where you are, geographically yes, mentally no, you are unsettled, we'll say, and then one day you walk into a place and say to yourself, 'if I had only known, this is where I belong.'

You roll up your sleeves and get down to work. Some have a great deal of 'it', and others have it so-so, almost everybody has some, and most of the best put their talent to work, if they recognize it and it is appreciated for what it is. Genius is something else again whether in large amounts or small, consistent or constant or interrupted. Some people know very early, and others learn it quite late in life when they are 'ready,' or confident is perhaps a better word. And I am a rich man not someone with any creativity or talent whatsoever, but I can recognize it when I see it. But you see, I know what I'm talking about, as this is my business. There are some people who are always creating, inventing, pursuing some dream or other, and many fall by the wayside while a few of the others succeed. There are only few who capture the essence of the age in a line or in a brushstroke. All the rest are mere imitators, copyists, people who love life as it is and wouldn't change it for the world, but oh, how boring," said Li laughing.

They went round looking at all the paintings and could easily see which were merely good from those that were great and those few monumental landscapes, which left one speechless.

"Here, a startled horse, look at his eyes! This man broke new ground every time he lifted an inked brush!"

Then one morning Rabi made his departure known to Guillaume by telling him that he was going to leave the following day, and if Guillaume had any letters for him to bring back to Andalusia he should write them the latest that evening. The next day Guillaume sought out Rabi, and gave him his letters to his parents, his bishop, Jacques, Al-Hakam and Hasdai.

He thought about Zara for a moment and then he quickly wrote her as well: I'm alive, and everything is fine and going my way, even though I'm writing these lines from China. I'll tell you all about it when I get back home. It shouldn't be more than a year from now, if everything works out well.

A few days later Solomon the pilot, the Persian captain came out of their cabins to meet with the ship's crew gathered on board. Then ship turned slowly around in the harbor and silently sailed off toward the Northeast. Guillaume was waving, and they all waved back.

Suddenly Guillaume felt alone again, just as he had known before, especially ever since Rabi had left the city two weeks ago.

He was really on his own. For the first time in China he looked around at the people, their houses and homes, their businesses, their Buddhist places of worship, and their food, their education process, and how they treated their children, how they related to one another, how they got along with one another. There was a good deal for him to absorb here. And he wanted to learn the language so that he could venture into the Chinese world himself, with its smell of ginger in the air. Still he was grateful that he had Wang as a translator.

The following day in Lu's office Guillaume was given some ginseng. Via the interpreter he was given to understand that it was a kind of "wonder" drug, curing many things and boosting the body's inner strength and sexual instinct, excellent also for the memory.

Guillaume thanked the man warmly as he had already thanked Wang Chou the go-between saying: "Without you this project would never be complete."

Wang Chou translated for him and Lu kept nodding his head with a big grin on his face.

"I'll give this, ginseng, much consideration, and I will want to take some back with me," said Guillaume.

The other men nodded, and they turned back to their work.

In time, Guillaume began seeing tiny needles within little cases around Lu's office and one day he asked him what they were for. Lu, through the interpreter, told him that this was a way of helping with acupuncture treatment. If Guillaume wished he to see for himself the use of acupuncture needles inserted into the skin at special places and learn about the results of numerous treatments.

When Guillaume had seen this art he wanted to be trained in it, and he told Lu. Lu informed him it would take a long time, but Guillaume persisted, and finally in order to avoid embarrassment, the Chinese doctor finally gave in.

They went on comparing medicines and drugs for several months until they had each exhausted their resources. Then came the final revision of their project in which each would have other doctors dispense their new drugs to see how they worked, what was the healing or cure rate or modification rate in a hundred patients for the first preliminary trials. As far as the doctors in China were concerned there was no need for preliminary trials as once the patient was cured or made better he, the patient, went home. For with the Chinese once a patient had been cured or helped he was released and no record was made or kept.

A few days later Lu began speaking about a disease, which had been cured called, "bad air". Guillaume said he had heard of such a disease before. Lu went on and Wang kept translating for Guillaume.

"It is put in hot water and a tea is made from it. In a week or a month a person is completely cured of sour air."

"May I have some of it to take with me and can it keep? It won't spoil will it?" asked Guillaume.

"Of course and it will keep indefinitely."

And the treatment for it was to take sweet wormwood and put it in hot water, lay it out after it has been infused and wait until the leaves were dried.

In a short period of time, a few doctors were participating in these trials having gotten somewhat excited about what was going on with this group of research physicians. And it began to spread to a few of the other doctors.

Guillaume decided to take a break after months of hard work of examining drugs for their affinities, differences, and active ingredients. Guillaume walked on toward his small house, and passed a public place, which featured Chinese music.

Several days later Guillaume met Wang and told him the trip to the interior of the kingdom was a dream he had, and he did not think it would be a good idea as he was going to continue with the acupuncture classes of Lu's doctor friend who was an expert in it. However, he was at a loss for someone to be able to teach him the Chinese, which he needed for acupuncture. Wang Chou wasn't doing anything at least until the start of next year when he had to go to the capital on business, and so he agreed to teach Guillaume both Chinese and acupuncture as far as he could.

Guillaume was thinking that he had wanted to learn the language as well as acupuncture, and he had a chance as long as the ship stayed away, but if the ship came back early his studies would be interrupted and he would have to leave. He had no idea how long it would take him to learn the rather complicated acupuncture treatment.

One afternoon Guillaume and Wang Chou decided to take a walk back toward the boats and junks on the water and as he got closer he could see the building of ships going on. It looked as though there were seventeen ships being built. The smoke and heat from fires used to soften the tar filled the air. The Chinese put tar on their boat bottoms to seal the wood against worms.

Guillaume couldn't understand why the Chinese wouldn't use the stars the way the Arabs did, especially since they were so good at star watching, and had such fine astronomers. Eventually he found out that they in fact did use astronomy.

They continued to walk on into town and stopped by an open-air eatery. Wang ordered for both of them. Guillaume did not know what the thin, cream-to-light-yellow colored rectangular shaped rubbery things were. So he asked Wang.

"Noodles, it's called noodles."

"I've been meaning to tell you, there is something called the 'Chunhuage Tie', which was created for the emperor. There was a gathering of many men's works from antiquity through the ninth century of 100 calligraphers, and their works were copied onto wooden blocks and then printed on paper. One of the finest calligraphers was named Wang Xizhi who lived in the 4th century. Each city was given one of them including the wooden blocks to make duplicates. And now Khanfu has had one for over a year. Today, almost everyone can now buy a copy for much less money than a hand printed one. It makes it easy to have a fine copy. You see?"

And Wang pulled out of his sleeve a copy of the 'Chunhuage Tie' and showed a page of it to Guillaume.

"I would be pleased to translate it into Arabic for you, if you would like to read it?" said Wang.

Guillaume had had no training in how to write Chinese calligraphy. But he had training in using brushes to write Andalusian Arabic and his calligraphy wasn't too bad, it was terrible. Other Arabs could actually read what he wrote and told him politely, that he wrote like a doctor writing prescriptions."

"That would be kind of you, how many volumes are in it or is it the only one?" asked Guillaume.

"Only eight.   Ready?" said Wang, indicating that he was ready to leave.

"Yes, oh no, that would be too much work for you, no. But thanks anyway."

"Actually, it would be a great treat for me, as it would help me to practice the calligraphy of the Arabs, and more importantly I could then have a man carve the wooden blocks, and set the wooden blocks to print my books and sell them if they were any good," said Wang.

"Yes," said Guillaume who didn't know what to say, whether to encourage or discourage Wang from his proposed work.

He didn't know if the man was being too polite or just saying what he did.   The Chinese were always so polite. So were the Arabs. One had to be careful in what one said to the Chinese and Arabs. For their languages tended to become flowery after hundreds of years. The Chinese can say, 'no' in the most beautiful of ways which often sounds like, yes.

Guillaume began thinking about translations. No translations, however good, can come close to the original. So truly, all translations are really lies, he concluded. And if all translations are lies then all translators are liars. Some translators are better liars than others. And then there are the funerals. If only the dead could hear the lies being told about them from friends of enemies or enemies of friends. It would make one cringe.

Wang and Guillaume became fast friends bantering all afternoon long about nothing. Then Wang began to get serious. He started telling Guillaume about the morning drum, which they heard every day and it seemed to be pounded endlessly in the market. Actually it was pounded 300 times in the morning, indicating that the market had opened, and another 300 times in the late afternoon when the market was supposed to close. But it seemed as though the markets never closed and went on with trading all night long.

"And speaking of plants which you are fond of, there was a man by the name of 'Camel Kuo,'" said Wang, "this man was a hunchback of Ch'ang-an, he grafted a peach branch to a persimmon tree. And he brought forth the golden peaches of Samarkand where he lived. This brought the patronage, as the tree lived and produced, of the wealthy in the capital. Everyone had to have one. A book entitled, The Book of Planting Trees, authored by

Camel T'o became very successful for it had the name of the man Camel Kuo in it. Unfortunately, this is a fabrication for this book was written in our dynasty, the Sung. Such is the greed, and deceit of the men of Han.   And it is not known how long the golden peaches of Samarkand have been in our country.   It is really indicative of the exotic tastes for articles and things from the outside world. Have you gone to the foreign section of town to the Arabs and Persians and looked in their gardens?"

Wang was a good speaker, and he was getting better by the day. His Arabic was becoming smooth and silky yet strong, and Guillaume liked listening to him. He liked learning from Wang. It was easy. Except when he got too excited then his Arabic became corrupted and he even came to saying a few words in Chinese in a high pitched and fast voice.   At that point Guillaume simply let Wang go on and laughed until Wang got red in the face and embarrassed himself. At that point Wang calmed down, and sheepishly slowed down as well.

"Anyway," he continued, the golden peaches came across the deserts of Serindia and were transplanted in Ch'ang-an in the orchards to become acclimatized."

"How do you happen to come by all that information, Wang?"

"My family has been in that business for three hundred years, Guillaume, we starved to come up with the money to buy, being the first to buy and sell the merchandise from the fleets of ships and because the trade has fallen off somewhat I and some of the other members of my family had to go into different professions, which is partly the reason I speak Arabic so well. All my family speaks this language."

"You would have thought that we would have had a trade imbalance with all our gold going out. But we had silk, tons and hundreds of tons, thousands of tons of silk worth its weight in gold coming back in, yes, we had the experience and fullness of time, time to create the finest silks in the world with the finest patterns, so the imbalances stayed fairly small. You must go to the Huangpu District where the Arabs are living. It is just to the right as the harbor opens up. And pay homage at the Nanhai temple there. All mariners go there and pray before they ship out."

"That's all right Wang, but I'm a Christian."

"Yes, but you must see it and I'll go with you if you like?"

"Very well, we'll go tomorrow."

"That's fine."

"Since you wanted me to see it, I must ask you why you want me to see it?"

"I simply wanted to see your reaction to it, to see how you would react, and the gardens," Wang said.

Guillaume nodded.

The following day they wandered through the districts by carriage looking at the gardens. Finally they came to Nanhi temple, the South Sea temple. Guillaume and Wang descended from the carriage and went inside, looking around and marveling at the structure. The temple was a sacred space in which anyone could pray. It was gaudy, thought Guillaume, with the vermilion pillars, the greens, blues, and yellows. It certainly stood out.

Guillaume chuckled at the place, and Wang noticed this, turned his head toward Guillaume and nodded.

"Well," said Guillaume, "I've seen this temple of yours but I've also seen the Huangpu, and I suggest we go back out another way taking the less traveled road back home, so that I might see the backyards of their homes. It looks as though some of our men are out planting more trees, and making a permanent residence here."

"Yes, we can certainly do that," and Wang gave orders to the driver.

In the back lanes of the houses Guillaume and Wang were able to see the perfectionism the owners had put their landscapes to in various styles, some Chinese and some Arabic. But all with various figs, cherry, plum, apricot, orange, peach, apple, and many other fruit trees in groves of orchards. Each attractive in various ways, there were little parks here and heavily forested areas there. These orchards contained much more than Guillaume had in his native northern home country.

Riding on they passed many magically manicured gardens, which looked quite natural. They continued further under the shade of overreaching trees interlocking each other down the lane. After a while the gardens all seemed to be the same within certain boundaries as if someone could go just so far in their gardening and no further. And then they were out of the wealthy district and into the much larger section where poorer people lived. Here everything was smaller and more hurried. The gardens merely copied one another. Finally the surroundings began to look familiar, they were back.

The days began to slide by for Guillaume as he continued his work. And then one day he saw what he thought was a girl he once knew. But he wasn't sure, as there were two of them. They were matched twins and coming closer to Guillaume on the lane he could see that they were also wearing matched silk dresses with a strange pattern on them.

"Quin Li?" said Guillaume hesitatingly first looking at one then another girl.

The girls laughed nervously as if there were a great secret amongst them.

"Quin Li, or is it Su Lee?" said Guillaume again, a little weaker this time.

Then the girls each raised a finger and wagged it in gesture from the left to the right several times in unison. And then they laughed at what they had done indicating that trying to address them was not customary in public especially on a street. They both giggled and ran away. Guillaume stood there and was completely stumped. He knew why they giggled, but not why they ran away. He did not follow them, for he knew he would see her again.

Underneath a colorful paper umbrella coal black eyes were seen that glistened from the sun, skin so unblemished with lips, so inviting a smile, so welcoming with blowing hair in gentle breezes and an invitingly lush mouth and then suddenly gone in an instant. He was spellbound for a few moments. Then Guillaume began to go into a strange trance, but it quickly faded from him for he had other things to do. Shaking his head he recovered himself.

A few days later Wang sought Guillaume out, and asked him if he was willing to go and see part of his family, among them a Taoist monk.

"What is a Taoist?"

"A Taoist is a religious man," said Wang. "You'll have to meet him, and ask him yourself."

"What is his name?"

"Ts'ao T'ang.

"I'll be glad to meet him," Guillaume said.

In the coming days Guillaume continued walking in the evening after work. He liked to walk up the river past the narrows where the bridge was, and the men in their boats polling them slowly along. Fishermen were walking home with their daily catch. They took him for a foreign sailor. One of the young women in a carriage dropped her folded paper umbrella nearly in front of Guillaume, the carriage stopped, and the young lady flipped it making sure it fell in front of him, gasping. Guillaume picked it up, and gave it back to the young lady and dropped his head toward her as was customary in those times.

Passing the bridge again it seemed smaller than in the daylight. And the crowds slowly thinned out except for those who were selling some items in little covered stands along the way. There were a few vendors selling liquor this early in the evening, and eventually Guillaume turned and walked up to one getting in line. When his turn came he ordered some rice and at another vendors' stand some rice wine. He sat down in a chair opposite an old Chinese man whom he saluted.

The old man nodded his head: "I see you are from around here."

Startled, Guillaume said: "Eh, yes, I live in a cottage up the road."

"I've seen you before and heard you speaking Arabic which I know. I'm also a retired physician, and a linguist, but I am from just over the hill, just there," the doctor said.

"Do you happen to know anything about Taoism?" asked Guillaume.

"I do. You see, I am also a Taoist."

"I'm Tu Kuang-t'ing, Doctor Tu Kuang-t'ing, physician to the court here in Khanfu, retired. I've been watching you for a while, and I could see that you weren't merely a sailor but someone of perhaps a more noble birth for a foreigner. So what brought you here?"

"Well, it's a long story, but the reason I'm here is to study medicine in all its different branches in various countries," laughed Guillaume.

"Well, I wish you all the luck in the world, young man. Perhaps we will meet again," said the old man as he got up from his chair in the tiny restaurant by the river, getting ready to leave.

"Goodbye and I also wish you very well."

The old man with very white hair and slightly crippled legs slowly walked away, he turned around, and waved back at Guillaume, and he waved back to him. Guillaume after having finished his rice and rice wine also departed and slowly walked home.

Opening the door to his cottage he found it very dark inside. He made his way over to the candle on his table, and lit it. The candle made a full circle of light not covering everything, but still enough to see with, and he went to bed because he was tired.

The next morning after he'd gotten up and got dressed Guillaume found a note slipped under his door.

It said: You are expected for dinner at the house of the Marquis of Chou next Sunday at eight in the evening.

Then there was a knock on his door.

Guillaume went to open it, and Wang came in saying: "Good morning."

"Good morning."

"Did you get my note?"

"Yes!"

"I'll come around in the evening to pick you up on Sunday."

"Yeah, that'll be fine."

"I'll see you then."

"A Marquis?"

"That's right, bye."

"Bye, see you later."

A few days later on Sunday evening Wang stopped by to pick Guillaume up, and after hiring a carriage Wang directed the man to his home.

They walked for a while until they came up to the landing, and started up the stone stairway. And inside, servants were coming and going bringing candles, and eating utensils and napkins, and porcelain containers, soups, meats and fish, and rice, with copious amounts of rice wine.

Wang motioned Guillaume into the study to meet his family, where his dad was snoring, and his mother was doing a little knitting. His mother woke up Wang's father, who looked around, and seeing a foreigner in his midst looked at his son before saying hello. Their daughters, whom Guillaume recognized as Quin Li and her twin Su Li which surprised Guillaume by being there also looked a bit concerned but said nothing.

"Hello," said Guillaume, to Wang's father, the Marquis.

"Hello, how are you? We've heard so much about you from Wang."

Guillaume looked a bit sheepish.

Wang said: "I'm hungry."

"So am I," said Guillaume.

Their meal was a very pleasant one with everyone making jokes and laughing softly under the tension.

And then in walked Ts'ao T'ang, the Taoist, who said: "Hello, hello, hello, am I late, again?"

"No, you're not too late for dinner, uncle Ts'ao," squealed his young niece.

Then Wang introduced Guillaume to Ts'ao.

The company and meal was pleasant and then uncle Ts'ao stood up whirled his cloak.

"I'm off."

And he disappeared leaving his cloak to fall on the rug covering the wooden floor.

"Oh, think nothing of it, Guillaume, he does it all the time, that trick is older than Buddha. After all, he's an alchemist, and Taoists do those strange kinds of things. He's probably in the kitchen right now eating leftovers."

And Guillaume was sitting in his seat looking at the goings on. Suddenly out of nowhere, a scented silky mist descended, and out of a perfumed dust swirl stepped Ma Ku as if in a dream, and she put her arm around Guillaume who looked up at her, and shrank back from this young woman who looked like an apparition.

And the lady said: "Hello, Guillaume, it is such a pleasure meeting you."

She spoke in the sweetest voice and tone he'd ever heard with her knee touching Guillaume's body. He didn't know what to say for once.

"You are very welcome here, Ma Ku Yen. Please sit down."

Guillaume grabbed a chair for her before Wang could do so, and placed it between them, he was in a jaw-dropping fascination with her. Ma Ku Yen smiled at Guillaume, and then at Wang, but she was certainly more interested in Guillaume and he was so surprised and unsure of himself that he didn't say a word.

"Are you my blue lad from beyond the Cyan Sea?" asked the charming lady speaking to Guillaume.

"I suppose so, I don't know."

Ma Ku Yen giggled and with her leg touching his, blinked her almond eyes lovingly with a shining smile, looking Guillaume over, and leaning to him to smell his scent. Then said goodbye and suddenly changed into a bird-woman, and flew off to the mystic isles. And Guillaume's mouth hung open in astonishment.

"Well, that was a short visit," said Wang's father. "What did you think of her?"

"I think I shall never see a young girl as pretty as she, like a bouquet of scented flowers slipping in a summer afternoon's breeze."

"She's not that young, young man, she's older than oldness itself," said Ts'ao T'ang coming up unsteadily from the downstairs wine cellar with a wine bottle hanging from his hand, "and the longer you look at her the older she gets", he said.

"I just look at her with one eye," said Guillaume.

Wang replied: "Well, her one eye is certainly looking at you."

And everyone immediately broke up laughing as though they couldn't help themselves.

Guillaume was completely dumbfounded.

"Oh, that's nothing, Guillaume, you dreamed it all. Didn't you know that, it was all imagined, but we were all dreaming the same thing. That's what Taoists do, they like to tease you, work you up, and put you into a trance, only he put us all in a trance, all at once."

"Really?" said Guillaume.

Guillaume was formally introduced to Qing and Su Li's, and as Ma Ku had left such an impression on him that he thought or imagined that he saw the same thing in the eyes of Qing and Su. He held their hands in greeting a bit too long and made the girls wrinkle their foreheads, smile and giggle in embarrassment.

Guillaume nodded and thanked them all for an interesting evening, a lovely dinner, and what people!

Wang and Guillaume didn't speak very much on the way back into town.

When the carriage stopped in front of Guillaume's cottage he got out.

Wang said: "I'm sorry you had such a lousy time, Guillaume."

"No, no, I had a wonderful time."

"Oh, I'm so glad, I thought you were unhappy or something."

"No, I wasn't unhappy, simply astounded, and your sisters, Su Li an Qing Li, I know Su Li or is it Qing Li, anyway, one of them came to our Chinese host's home once when we were dressed like Chinese and sang a beautiful song to us, told us about the monkey king, and a story about how Li Po died."

"Ah, yes, but their last name in Chinese is pronounced Lee not Li and the story about Li Po is, well, it is strictly fictitious. The story was made up simply to boost his reputation, but his story is much more than that, you see. He was initiated into the Taoist system."

"Goodnight."

"Goodnight."

Guillaume went into his cottage, lit his candle and began to get undressed. He lay down on his bed, and thought about the evening at Wang's home, in fact he couldn't stop thinking about it. Everything was a bit confused in his mind. Eventually, he rolled over on his side, and fell asleep, lightly at first then into a very deep sleep in which he was being pulled by someone's hand in the darkness. But he couldn't see who it was, then, he looked up and saw that it was Ma Ku Yen smiling at him, and with her other hand she was motioning for him to come with her. He wasn't sure where she wanted to take him, and he began resisting her, but in the end he had to go with her. And she took him into the gaps, the space between things, which were rarely ever seen in daylight life. For he seemed to be in the middle of something he didn't know. Except that as he saw things they began to slow down, and in that darkness he saw Ma Ku Yen. Then in the darkness there were lights, colored lights. And then the music began and it went on and on and it all began to twist faster and faster down a hole. First large then small, but always Ma Ku Yen was pulling him with her with her almond eyes and after a while it all slowed down. Guillaume found himself in the sky standing on an island suspended in the sky with Ma Ku Yen.

"This is where I live," but she didn't say it, her mouth was closed, and Guillaume flinched when he realized he was reading her sensations of colored-vibrations, which came out of the top of her head, and spread up and out behind her like a beautiful fountain.

"It is very beautiful here, but so lonely. And for that reason I go back down to the earth, and bring someone like you up here to come, and play with me now and then," she said. "Won't you relax now, and walk with me in my island above the Cyan Sea, and later I will make you partially forget that I brought you up here, but you will have great creativity within you for a little while as a lasting gift from me, only you will not remember where it came from. One day you will suddenly discover it in yourself, and it will help you in whatever you do."

She laughed now, and they began to play little games, children's games in the sky, seek and find. And finding her he enclosed her in his arms, kissing her and falling into the pools of her almond eyes. Hearing her laughter, and again, kissing her warm lips he became entangled in her soft black Oriental hair. He kissed her cheek, her lower neck and touched her full breasts. And gently, yes, she gave in.

Guillaume suddenly woke up. Something or someone had tapped his window. A bird? Children playing? He didn't know what it was, and in any case, it meant nothing to him, he got up and drank a glass of water. He remembered something of his dream. Some flying thing, bright lights and music, which he had never heard before, and the face of someone he knew, Su Li? Guillaume was tired and couldn't remember any more. Rolling over he went back to sleep. And once again he was in the fields running with his dogs, Duke and Duchess under a clouded sky through the tall grasses bringing home the fool's gold he'd found, his treasure he had wanted to give to his parents. But every time he tried to give them something, something stopped him. Some darkness.

And then he was away again. But it was futile for the dream he wanted to remember was gone. In his restlessness Guillaume turned over and finally, it was time to get up. Guillaume got dressed most unwillingly and sat there on his bed trying to piece together what he had dreamed, but to no avail. He only managed to recall some fragments.

Guillaume went to the little Chinese stand he had gone to the other night, and ordered his noodles and sitting down he noticed that the old retired doctor was sitting next to him.

"Good morning."

"Good morning to you, Dr. Guillaume," replied the old man.

"May I ask you a few questions about Taoism?" Guillaume turned to Dr. Tu.

"Of course, you may," said Dr. Tu pleasantly.

"Are people or can people truly be put in trances?"

"Oh, yes."

"Trances where you are awake, and can see and hear?"

"Yes, of course, but there is also a matter of drugs which a Taoist often indulges in."

"In a family's home I saw Ma Ku Yen, and a night later I saw her in a dream."

"Did she say anything? What did she say?"

"She seemed to be interested in me, for some reason."

"Was there a Taoist present?"

"Yes, there was," said Guillaume.

"I think the man, the Taoist, was just playing a joke on you, earning his supper, so to speak."

"And the woman?" asked Guillaume.

"Ma Ku Yen?"

"Yes."

"You know, these adepts like to use all kinds of things to fool people, to enhance their reputation, like putting certain kinds of mushrooms in your food, to give you hallucinations, to make you see things, which really aren't there, and blowing smoke in people's eyes. That kind of thing that is their magic."

"No, he wasn't an adept. He was a full-blown Taoist of the Mao Shan."

"Well, I think he was just having fun, but those things can be rather powerful, you know, they can put people in trance without even trying, make them believe certain things, that reality is something different from what it is, it isn't something to worry about," said Dr. Tu.

"But what I saw..."

"What you saw were grottoes, island utopias in the airy distance, and palaces of the skies, cloud palaces, pure fantasies."

"Yes, that kind of thing."

"But what you saw was of the imagination, hallucination, extreme day-dreaming, eroticism, reverie, again these things are the playthings of the Taoists."

"I sure had a strange and clear dream that night. Thank you very much, Dr. Tu, I may have more questions for you again in the future."

"Yes, certainly."

Guillaume stood up paid his bill and left.

And Dr. Tu sat there and thought: "Perhaps I have confused him into thinking that it was all in the imagination, and not real. Perhaps he will now forget about it?"

But Guillaume didn't forget about Ma Ku Yen. He couldn't. He began obsessing about her. He thought about nothing else. In his rich imagination he was entangled with her on a floating bed of softened pink tinged-blue white clouds with the bright flashing sunlight streaming in the timeless afternoon as he made love again and again with her whispering and saying: "Yes, oh, yes!"

He tried to get her completely out of his mind. He began thinking about an old woman he had seen that early morning with many lines, and creases down her face having a struggle in walking slowly along the street, and having no teeth, but who kept turning into the beautiful and ageless Ma Ku Yen in his mind.

Then Guillaume not getting anywhere with his vision of Ma Ku Yen, began cartwheeling along the street. Suddenly three young girls saw this behavior and unexpectedly burst out giggling and laughing in a manner in which they were not taught.

And then he started running with all his might up a tiny very steep hill and with the momentum he managed to come full circle around, and back on his feet. By this time he was so out of breath that his hyperventilating caused him to forget her.

"Finally," he said, "I'm free. I'm free."

Then he started thinking about her again as soon as he caught his breath and this made him melancholy. Finally, he really did manage to forget her when thinking about his plants. And he realized that he hadn't gone to work for several days. He wondered if Wang was still there or had returned home.

Eventually he went back to work losing himself in it until the only things he thought about were plant technology and how to decide what strengths could he use as a way of listing plants. He decided that he needed something to tell what strength an ingredient could be before it was called a poison or a treatment. He thought it would vary from patient to patient. Some patients could take more, and some less for the same effect. A heavier person would take more, and a skinny person less. All he could do was try, and hope that he didn't kill anybody.

He went to work that day, but found that Wang had not been there for several days, so he said goodbye to Lu and went back out leaving Lu a bit disconcerted.

A few days later Wang came looking for Guillaume and found him at home.

"Ah, there you are, I've been looking for you all day at Lu's office, at your cottage, everywhere."

"Are you ready to go to work?"

"Oh, yes, I'm ready, shall we go now?" asked Wang.

"Yes."

A storm suddenly broke out and the rain came down blindly hard. So they hailed a covered cab, and drove to the office. Getting out they laughed at how wet they were. Soon they were up in Lu's office and Lu was excitedly telling Wang the latest news he'd found out.

Guillaume was shaking out his clothes, and listened to Wang relate the news of the plants, the tree gum, and the bark. For the Chinese had not thought much of them. Lu had a list of drugs, which he then tried on patients, and they had seemed to work a little better than the ones he was used to. However he had to be careful with the dosage as too much would undo all the help he had done. So his experiments were made slowly and carefully and it all had to be written down in Chinese and Arabic.

So his trip to the land of the Han, as the Chinese called themselves, was not entirely wasted particularly when he witnessed the treatments given by physicians of two other cultures. His knowledge and experience began to deepen.

And he started to feel himself and his experiences move from a doctor's status to a physician's perspective. It was not a line that had to be crossed it was simply a different perspective, a growing perspective in one's mind. And he felt particularly proud of his progress in acupuncture until his Chinese acupuncture doctor explained that he had merely passed the first part of twelve parts of the course. This sobered him up.

One morning Guillaume went to the office and Dr. Win Shu was there, greeting him warmly. Shu and Lu were engaged in excited talk, their speech so fast that Guillaume couldn't follow it.

"You see", said Win Shu, "it was the Koreans who developed acupuncture first, and we who developed it after, quite independently."

Win Shu had been able to bring a great quantity of plants back with him, so many in fact, that the majority were still on board of the ship. The following morning Guillaume and Win Shu pushed the Arabian skiff out to the ship and once on board met Solomon and various crewmembers.

Win Shu told Guillaume about the point where ships to Korea were crowded together. The Arabs had many of their supplies and residences there. They had found Korea welcoming and profitable and so were disposed to stay in a small colony there and married some of the local women. Most of the plants were very similar to plants growing in China, but not all.

Guillaume and Win Shu took all the plants off the SeaWolf and bade Solomon goodbye. The crew simply wanted to do nothing better than to sleep.

Win Shu talked to Guillaume about Taiwan, a rather large island off the coast of China and directly northeast of them. The island's spine was right down the middle with rugged mountains towards the eastern seaboard, while on the western side mountains sloped downwards towards the sea. There were aborigines living there with blue tattoos who couldn't speak any of the languages that the men could. Even sign language seemed too complicated for them.

Win Shu had listed all the plants in a particular order in his notebooks and so he unloaded the carriage himself. They went over all the plants and how they had to be watered, some more than others. Guillaume was impressed and well paid the doctor for his efforts. Dr. Shu was happy that everything turned out so well. He now had a little money to find an office to lease and a little experience as a ship's doctor. Guillaume too was pleased. He asked Win about Japan and he said the people there were not exactly built like Chinese. And Win began telling Guillaume about incense, which the Japanese had made into an art form which seemed to cure certain illnesses.

Win spent hours explaining to Guillaume all the things he learned.

HOME

The ship was turned over, placed upright as well as the other smaller vessels, pushed into the water and the reloading began. When this was done the men waited for the tide to change before getting into the ships and they were off to sailing to the East. They went around the island and then northwest up the tail.

Coming to the land again they turned the ships in the opposite direction. Then they went nearly west.

This entire sailing, passing of islands gradually made sense to them. Solomon knew that had he not gone from island to island he could have completely missed the ones he was looking for. Having gotten out his old maps, which placed him at the extreme last position he had sailed once before, he spent an inordinate amount of time on them.

He waited and waited and then one day he sailed down the western side of this island and the length of it seemed to him to fit the map. Then another island, and another and another, and he knew he was on the right course. Weeks and weeks of sailing had gone by before he was sure.

"Now we are definitely on our way home".

It seemed like the best news the crew had had for a long time. They were ecstatic and their emotions exploded over everything they tried to say. And then something else exploded. It completely took them by surprise. Red-hot rocks went whistling by and plunged into the sea. They didn't know what was happening. The sky was darkening grey and black with clouds. At first they thought the sea was on fire. But as that was impossible, yet it was what they saw. And seconds later it didn't seem to matter for the ship was in trouble and floundering.

The men were staggering across the deck and some were shouting: "Ya Rahman, oh Merciful One."

The sea became much rougher now with giant waves washing the men off the deck and onto the ropes, which helped them to save themselves. But Guillaume kept sliding and eventually fell off the ship.

"Help, help me," screamed Guillaume, spitting out some seawater. "Somebody, help!"

He went down under the black swirling sea into the darkness, where his hearing was muffled. The bubbles quickly came up and disappeared. He could see very little and heard nothing at all. The darkening sky on the horizon was claiming the light of the day. And Guillaume was drowning.

The volcano kept spewing out black and dark-grey smoke and fire and hundreds of small fireballs and the light began to fade quickly. Then another round came bursting out of the exploding volcano. The water shook several times sending large ripples and then waves.

The men were looking over the side of the ship. Others looked up to see the fiery red sparks which seemed like boulders when coming at them and suddenly hitting the water. Then they sent huge plumes of seawater over all around them. The men were busy for one of the hot bursts had hit and gone through one of the sails. It was dropping on deck and starting a fire. They were busy throwing seawater on it.

Guillaume was still struggling frantically and he couldn't think how to swim the way Solomon had tried to teach him. And he went down again, deeper this time.

"Somebody help me! Oh, God, please," and he went under again, "don't let me die here like this!"

Down he went and bubbles were coming up. When he came up the ship had been floundering and twisting back and forth and the side of the ship and Guillaume collided. And he went down again as the ship closed over him.

After struggling until his strength was gone he was going down for the third time, and coming up. And the ship hit him broadside along his back, which made him vomit up the seawater that had gone into his lungs and belly. Guillaume finally touched something with his big toe, which he scraped with his toe, and the sharpness of the pain made him swim harder until he found solid ground. Exhausted he pulled himself up on to the sand in the dead of night and passed out.

In the morning the half-drowned man lay shivering in the early light while a crab was flipping Guillaume's eyelid with one of its arms. Guillaume closed the eyelid, which the crab was interested in and opened his other eye, but his sight wasn't clear. The crab persisted. Finally Guillaume was able to sit up, and the crab backed up several feet and hissed at him while waving its front claw at him. Guillaume made a growling sound, and the crab scampered on tiptoes back.

He looked up, and saw the white sand extending all across the way along the atoll, and up to an island with trees and palms about a thousand yards long and wide. And then Guillaume found out that this was no atoll. The island had seven steep craggy hills fifteen feet high, and small sharply rough hills on it.   Guillaume stood up, and feeling sick again, he vomited up the last of the seawater. There were no ships anywhere in sight. It began to dawn on him that he was utterly alone. But he was alive.

"Oh, God," he looked at his feet and saw he had lost his shoes as they must have come off in the seawater.

His throat was cracked dry and he needed water. Guillaume looked around and seeing nothing struggled to walk up to the island. But the muscles in his legs wouldn't give him the strength he needed having exercised them far too much the previous evening and he fell. Then he became angry with himself for being in this situation.

"Why me, damn it, why me?"

He picked up an old seashell and threw it out into the sea as hard as he could which wasn't very far, and he fell down again weak with exhaustion.

Getting up again he walked slowly across the sandy beach looking out to sea and all around him. He saw nothing. No ships. Nothing.

Something in him told him to listen to his mind's ear, and he heard the voice of reason telling him that he was still alive and should be grateful. He was virtually undamaged, and healthy. And this made him think. For no matter how bad the situation was, he would think a way out of it or be reconciled to his disaster. He needed water to wash out the seawater, which cracked his throat.

After walking across the beach he reached the land in which life had found a niche, and climbed up onto the grasses that bound the island together. Walking a little further up the turf he found a tiny natural pond with yellowed grasses nearly covering it, and with fairly clear rainwater in it.

He fell down again in his haste to drink it, hitting his head on some large rocks, and fainted again.

When he woke up his head hurt him and he was bleeding, but his throat bothered him the most. He cupped his hand in the water, and splashed it on his face, and cupped his hands again and drank a little. He did this several times.

Guillaume was feeling a little better, and he began to look around to try to find something to eat. The island contained palm trees, the male, and the female, plenty of them. It meant something to eat. He knew this because one of the men had told him about being shipwrecked on an island with nothing but coconuts to eat, and how to break them open, and how to eat them after drinking the juice inside. So he set to work gathering up coconuts finding a thick branch with a sharp edge on it, and pounded it into the ground. Then he sharpened the ragged edge with a rock as best he could and proceeded to break open the coconut by smashing it downward on the stick. Some of the coconuts were old and dried up, and the hardened milk inside had gone bad. These he threw to one side.

And then one moment he broke open a coconut, which had liquid inside and he spilled all that precious liquid on the ground. But he saved a little of it and drank his fill of the soft, white, solid milk inside. He continued to get better at breaking open the coconuts until he could split one nearly in half. After a while he felt better, and relaxed against a tree.

For three days he did this, and then one day he saw a ship. No, it was two ships in the distance. And they were coming toward him. He was jumping up and down, waving his arms, and shouting excitedly.

"Hey, look, over here, over here!"

But the ships kept going, and the direction they were coming from they would be going past him. He took off his shirt, and began waving it. Then he put it on a long stick and waved it.

Finally, after a time, one of the ships broke off its course, and began coming straight at him. Then the other ship as well. Now Guillaume was really jumping up and down in an irregular pattern on the sand waving his shirt wildly and laughing until he fell down from exhaustion. Panting, he lay there trying to catch his breath, and continued to wave his shirt slower and closer to the ground. And then he felt faint, but did not pass out from the exertion. The last thing he remembered was looking up at his flag in the sky, and everything nearly went black as he collapsed into the warm comforting sand.

The longboat ran aground in the soft white sand of the atoll, with the palm trees leaning outward and smaller bushes crowded round. Other men found the coconuts and Guillaume, who had collapsed from exhaustion, yet he was awake and they gently carried him to the long emergency boats.

They were quite happy to find him having looked for three days. Their largest ship had burnt and sunk.

Guillaume didn't wake up until the evening, and when he did he lay on his back looking up, seeing the pilot looking down at him.

"Thank God, we've found you, and you are in one solid piece," said Solomon. "And a little hungry, too?"

"Oh, yes", he said weakly, "I can smell the rice, and I can only think of how sweet it will taste."

"Well, that old rice will be warmed up a little more in a minute or two. Can you sit up Guillaume?"

"Yes, I think so, but I am terribly tired."

"You should be, three days without much in your system except coconuts, but they can last you awhile, and you have very little fat on you to lose, here is the rice now, careful don't burn yourself."

"Yes, thank you!"

"You should have seen that fire. Smoking and burning sails, then the decks on fire, and all the bags of pepper, with their watertight containers filled with air floating on the seas as they were all attached to one another, spilling over the side of the ship. We lost four men that night, but got the pepper, and I saved all my papers and books."

"Bad night, that night."

"Two were Arabs, one Indian, and the Malayan, all good men. And I lost my astrolabe."

"And I mine, too, and a few books I picked up in Alexandria."

"I've never lost my ship before, but it was unavoidable. At least there wasn't much cargo lost."

"No one could have known about that volcano. No one lived on that island for the very reason that it was smoking."

"We should have known better, as we had seen other volcanoes smoking away before."

"We should have sailed away from it the moment I saw what was turning the evening's sky black. Well, that's all past now.

We've saved our skins, and with what we saved of our cargo we'll be all right, and out of the profits I can supply the stricken families with enough income to supply their yearly needs," continued Solomon.

Guillaume ate his rice and now and then nodded his head.

"I can see that we're pretty crowded now, having divided the men between the two other ships," said Guillaume.

"Yes, that's why we settled on three ships just in case something like this happened," added the pilot, "and we were lucky."

Guillaume strained to sit up, but Solomon pushed him back down again, and said: "You're not ready yet, eat your rice, relax, and sleep, the men can wait."

"Yeah, I am so tired and weak, I wouldn't be any good trying to help anyone else right now."

So Guillaume slept the sleep of the dead not dreaming of anything or anyone, slowly healing his mind and body.

The next day he was able to sit up, and even get up for a few minutes, but as his legs felt rubbery underneath him. He knew it was time for him to rest further. His balance was also off.

The third day came and went without much strength in him. He ate twice as much as he was used to, and late in the afternoons he drank a little rice wine. Slowly feeling better over the days he was capable of getting up again and move around a little. He took a critical look at the seamen who were lying on deck in their misery, drinking all the rice wine they could, some of them completely drunk. A few of the more religiously inclined did not drink at all.

He pulled the legs of two of the crewmen resetting their bones, while another far more sober sailor held the man, and once his leg was in place he got some simple timber and made splints with a hand axe putting one on one side and another one on the other side. All the while he was wrapping the man's leg with the help of the sailor who had been looking after the men. Then he looked at the men with broken arms who had been there all night, with one man's bones coming through the skin.

Guillaume had the man drink more wine until he was nearly stupefied and as the sailor was holding him, Guillaume gave a jerk, and the man passed out but with his arm in place. And with two splints underneath the wrapping Guillaume had put on him.

The men with their hips broken would just have to lie still for six weeks.

Gradually Guillaume regained his strength and while doing so helped out the sick, as well as the men with broken bones. In time, Guillaume gained the respect of these men for he took care of them in a loving way. And the men didn't have to work, as there was a surplus of men now after the loss of one ship. So Solomon broke the crews into various sections, with some on day duty and some off for the night.

There was now hardly enough work for all the men and the pilot set the men to repairing the ships. This work gave them something to do to keep their minds off the calamity that had just happened.

The black men from Sudan swam down taking a look at the underside of the ships, while others manned the pumps getting the last of the water overboard. There were few cracks or holes in the planking, but enough seawater was coming in to justify a look. The easy-going black men were smiling in the knowledge that they were needed worked away sealing what they thought were tiny holes, and after a while the men who were working the pumps could relax for the water stopped coming in.

Then the men began to put patches on the sails, where the burning boulders had flown through. And the ships began to get underway, slowly at first, but then with greater speed for the wind had come up. Thank Allah, the rudder held. And soon in the dying daylight the sails dried and began snapping with the wind. These great lateen sails all triangular-shaped billowed out with the wind and they were flowing along again, cutting larger and larger troughs in the sea. The men started smiling and talking, commenting on the wind.

Guillaume sat near the railing of the ship letting his hair dry in the wind. He felt good to be alive and he was hungry. In time, the cook made dinner cooking up the rice, which they had at every meal and some fish. The fish had been gutted and sprinkled with salt. Also a giant tortoise had been found, caught and gutted. Its innards were cooked in the shell like a stew. Almost any change of food was welcome by the sailors.

They thought about their wives, their children, and sweethearts when the winds were slaking off, and they were still in the water with a number of men in the longboats slowly pulling the ship into the trade winds. It had been a long voyage, longer than any of them had known.

Guillaume thought about his brother Jacques, and then his parents, and Zara. He had not written a letter since leaving China. There was no mail service out here, because there was not a trace of civilization in this area. They were cut off and all very much alone at the end of the world.

They continued sailing north for the coral was too close to the surface of the water and there was only one or two breaks in that chain the entire length along the coast.

Now the sky had darkened and they were unable to see the stars. They could not move far without losing their last navigational location.

They next day they set a course to the West and sailed on for 400 leagues. They continued until they found two islands, both relatively northward and parallel, but not the same size. Then they saw another more distant oblong island.

From there they sailed another 100 nautical leagues in two days to get to the lower leg of Kele Island. Then they went in a southwesterly direction until they saw an island chain about 120 nautical leagues south of them. Following this they sailed in a westerly direction until they came to Java and stopped at the northern side near Jaca.

The men relaxed coming upon friendly and charming people, and Guillaume used the opportunity to take time off and go looking in the markets where he found a shaman who could understand some Arabic. Guillaume asked him if he knew of any incense, which would comfort the stomach, strengthen the limbs, and perfume the breath?

"Oh, yes! We have that."

Guillaume bought a couple of bundles of that particular incense.

Solomon could not afford to delay right now as he had calculated the distance to go with the number of days left for the monsoon blowing them home. And the days were growing shorter.

Under Solomon's orders the men backed the ships into the surf after only two days on shore and then put the ships into deeper water. Soon the ships propelled by a warm friendly wind began to sail on. Each day they covered a larger number of nautical leagues. The white water on the bow rose ever higher each day, meaning they were making faster and greater speed.

Eventually they saw the outline of the coast of India coming into view and later the next day dropped their sails and floated into their niche when they found Kerala. The palm trees swayed in the breezes coming from the sea. The sky was light blue and the sea dark green-blue and black. Guillaume remembered the last time he was here. The ship crunched up into the long dried grasses and the men jumped out, laughing all the way for they too remembered Kerala.

Solomon issued a few orders and the men quieted down. The second ship also crunched up into the grass. Solomon issued more orders to get several men together and go into the town nearby to get fresh water and some different food to resupply the ships. The rest of the men were glad to have an opportunity to relax from their work on board, languidly slept, or indulged in small talk.

In the evening various carts with bulls pulling them came with water and food for the men, announcing their arrival by all the squeaking noise they made. Slowly the men got up and into the work, putting the barrels on board. This was difficult to do and time consuming as the ship had no pulley to pick up and bring supplies into the ship.

At dawn men began needling the cook to get him to warm up some of the food. They were pleased and afterwards had no qualms about pushing the ships back into deep water.

The fact was the men were more eager to leave than they were eager to stay and said their goodbyes.

They kept looking until the landscape grew smaller and thinner and then disappeared. The chickens squawked in their wooden cages in the front of the ship, letting the men know they were there. And when the wind switched directions and blew their awful smell back into their faces some of the men coughed. But Solomon wouldn't let them throw the birds into the sea. He told them that the chickens provided fresh eggs and when the hens were old they had roasted chicken meat to eat.

Sailing West Northwest they came up to the Tropic of Cancer and into the Gulf of Oman they sailed rounding the horn into the Persian Gulf. Now the men were truly happy for their homeland was within reach. A week later they were at Al-Basra.

They passed on their left sailing northward on the Tigris River. The tall palm trees on each side of them looked like sentinels following one another equally spaced a hundred feet apart with their life saving coconut milk and meat for needy travelers who met with unforeseen accidents and had lost their provisions.

Sailing further north the river became narrower and smaller until they reached Baghdad and each ship pulled into one of the slips.

Solomon got out his charts and motioned Guillaume to come with him. When they were up on the landing they could see the entire city.

Then Solomon and Guillaume went to an audience with the caliph. The caliph was thinking and could not make a decision. He saw Solomon and quietly made a few comments to one of his men at arms and was immediately put forward of all the others. He finished with the man who was ahead of Solomon and motioning for him to come closer. Solomon and Guillaume stepped forward and bowed.

"So," said the caliph in a stern manner, "I thought perhaps you had run away with all my jewels in your pockets."

"You play with me. You know better than that for I've had to kill men in the past for you," said Solomon.

"I know, I know. Tell me now of your voyage. After all, you've been gone for a very long time," said the caliph.

"Yes, I have. I've lost seven men and the great ship along with some materials."

"What happened?"

"That is a long story."

Solomon pulled his right hand towards him and looked at his silver ring with the inscribed Jewish Star of David. He pushed it and the ring flipped open. Solomon then took out of the inside some paper, which he unfolded and gave to the caliph.

The caliph looked at it for a moment and then motioned the guard over and said: "Take this and give it to my accounting department, to the head of it and he'll know what to do."

Guillaume had completely forgotten about the ring and its hidden lever, its message inside.

"Send these people to the dining room area and at least give them something to eat. I don't think standing around here all day is going to improve their attitude towards me," said the caliph, "and then we'll have more time to talk in the evening."

After the meal and a bath, as well as putting on fresh clothes given by the palace, Solomon told the caliph in the evening all the details about the voyage and Guillaume again was present. The caliph listened with interest.

Afterwards the caliph gave Solomon a couple of small diamonds and told him to buy another ship and stock it with his own valuables.

"Oh, thank you."

The caliph then took another large diamond out and gave it to him for his time and troubles in the East.

Solomon gasped.

"This young man here he looks different. Is he from somewhere in the North?" asked the caliph.

"Yes. He was a Benedictine monk who studied medicine in Cordoba, learned languages and wanted to know more. He was then ambushed off the coast north of Valencia by pirates, got wounded and nearly died. When he recovered he came by my ship through the recommendation of my cousin and this young man asked if I needed a doctor. I have liked his quickness and watched as he dealt with people and took responsibility, whether given to him or not, that I decided to teach him navigation so that today he is in reality a pilot, a junior pilot. Can you bestow on him the full rank of navigator?"

"Of course," said the caliph and signaled to a man at arms to come over.

He whispered something to him.

A few minutes later the man returned with his brush, ink, paper and cowhide and the caliph wrote everything out, drawing a dhow with letters and words in a fancy Kufic script.

"What is your name, young man?" asked the caliph.

"Guillaume de la Puy en Valey."

"How would one write that?"

"Oh", said Solomon, "like this."

And he wrote it out on the thick paper. Once it had dried was rolled up and tied in the middle the document was handed to Guillaume and the caliph pronounced with solemnity that he was now a navigator by this act of the caliph. Now he was a professional seaman.

Guillaume didn't have the faintest idea of what to do, so he awkwardly bowed to the caliph. The caliph said he'd keep the maps and indicated that the audience was over now.

When they were back at the ships, Guillaume pondered what he would do next. Solomon decided to get to Jeweler's street as fast as he could, dragging Guillaume along with him. He selected a good Jewish jeweler whom he knew as an acquaintance and put down on the counter the three diamonds, which the caliph had given him. And once that transaction had been completed Solomon also put down a small bag of gems.

"This goes to my Jewish community here in Bagdad. I must have the transaction finished before the caliph starts depressing the gems market by dumping all those jewels, and here is your portion, navigator, for having helped me to bring the ship home," said Solomon.

He put on the counter a small fortune in rubies, emeralds and diamonds. The jeweler again made the transaction for Solomon and gave Guillaume the money for them.

"I didn't know I was receiving a salary."

"You weren't, but I had to provide something for all the time that you were on board of the ship taking responsibility. And it looks to me as though you've earned a small fortune to replace what you lost and now you have a way home."

Guillaume happily put the cash into his pocket. Solomon thanked the jeweler and then took Guillaume down to the trader's street to find when the next camel caravan would leave for Beirut on the Mediterranean coast. Solomon made arrangements for Guillaume, who knew virtually nothing about prices and all the exact details.

"Whatever you are thinking is probably true, of course I didn't give to the caliph all the jewels because he regularly cheats and intimidates his men and me. And you have been given more than you are worth just to keep your mouth shut. And Guillaume, we have been lucky to get back alive from so long a trip."

"Ha", said Guillaume, "I am not going to pry into how and why you make your money, good sir, you know what you're doing."

It was now the afternoon by the time they were there looking at all the camels that had drunk the water and filled their humps out.

Whenever Solomon stayed in the Jewish community he spent the time in his house in Baghdad. It was filled with people and the remnants of his family, his wife had died years earlier, and without any children he grew restless for the sea where he could forget all his troubles in tending to the challenges ahead and it kept him quite fit.

Guillaume stayed on board of the ship that night and the next, as they had not found a slip where the shipyard men could work. It would take months to outfit a new ship. But Guillaume's mind wasn't set on any of that. He was thinking about when he was going to get home. Also he felt anxious about Jacques, his parents, Al-Hakam II, Zara and all the other people he began to remember.

Meanwhile quick as a wink, Solomon went around the jewelers asking about prices of jewels, knowing the caliph would dump on the market all those jewels and when the prices were dipping 2/3 he bought the jewels back all of which infuriated the jewelers.

Guillaume turned his attention toward getting ready to go with the caravan. That night when Solomon came back to the ship, Guillaume stepped out and embraced him.

"Solomon, I will always remember you."

"And I you," said Solomon. "Give me your address in Andalusia.

"I'd like yours too," said Guillaume writing in Latin. "I suppose there are ways to get past the censors on either side?"

"Yes, Guillaume, but it costs ten times as much, if you ask around, be discreet".

"That isn't going to be a problem for me."

In the evening Guillaume cleaned out his cabin and put everything in a bag, which he could carry.

Both Solomon and he awoke at dawn in preparation for Guillaume's leaving.

The camels all made disagreeable sounds in a cacophony of noise as if protesting what the camel master wanted them to do. Guillaume's camel rose in an unnatural swing and then waited for the other camels to finish their grumbling and get up and go.   Then the camel master started to walk and his camel behind him and the others following them in a line, which stretched a quarter of a league.

Guillaume looked back at the distant towers, large mosques, and all the movement stirred up the dust.

After a while all he could see were fresh camel tracks. He looked ahead into the desert. The monotonous rhythm began to tire him out and he slowly slipped into a long sleep.

It was dark when he awoke and the caravan had just stopped to allow the men to relieve themselves and prepare a meal. After eating the men introduced themselves. And the caravan master said that they would not go any further this day. The men got their blankets down from the camels.   Some of the men stayed up and looked at the stars in the sky, telling stories. One of the men pointed out the Pole Star, and the Plough, the Little Bear, and the constellations of Orion.   And when the last lantern went out the men could see the shooting stars.

It continued like that for the entire journey of that caravan until they arrived at the coast of Beirut. Guillaume immediately began to make arrangements for his clothing and goods in an inn in the Christian quarter of town and then hurried for the ship owners, asking if he and his goods could be taken to Spain.

Finally he found a ship owner who would take him as far as Nemesis in Cyprus and from there to the little port town of Timbukion in Crete, where he would have to get another ship to go further west. So he booked the passage to Crete.

Guillaume went back to the inn to relax in his room.

When he awoke it was still early enough to get something in the restaurant attached to the inn. He ate heartily, wiping his greasy hands on a piece of cloth provided by the establishment. Guillaume was finishing his chicken, when the fellow who sat down opposite began asking him questions.

Guillaume was happy to meet a fellow human being who wanted to talk that he forgot himself and told the stranger the particulars of his entire journey. The cook came by to pick up the empty dishes and while standing behind the stranger signaled to Guillaume, that he should stop talking to this man seated in front of him.

Guillaume understood the cook's head shaking and placing the finger to the lips, and he quickly changed the situation and stopped talking by putting an excess of food in his mouth. The man figured that Guillaume had suddenly sized him up and got up, paid and left.

"Don't you know that you can't talk to strangers around here?" said the cook.

"Sorry, I wasn't thinking clearly. I just got off a caravan from Baghdad and I'm pretty tired as I haven't had much sleep in a few weeks."

"You had better keep awake and alert around here."

Guillaume looked at the cook, nodded and expressed gratefulness for the good advice. He got up, paid and went to look around the neighborhood. The lanterns on the ships provided a little light, so too did the lanterns on the public buildings, which were still in business. He walked the wharf to the end, turned around and walked back up towards the restaurant. He wanted to see some more of the shop and bought some food for his journey.

Finally in mid-morning of the next day everybody was accounted for in the ship and the sails unfolded into bulging white, matching the clouds. And the ship slowly went west into the dark blue-green sea.

Cyprus was reached after only three days.

Within seconds the sails were trimmed by the pilot and slowed his ship down. They were at the port of Nemesis. At noon the next day they continued their journey and pushed off and sailed into a crosswind, now heading west for Phaestus in southern Crete.

In Phaestus Guillaume found another ship, which would take him further west.

The following morning the ship to the Emirate of Sicily sailed out of the harbor, while the seagulls looking for tidbits from the passengers screeched and screamed. Getting nothing from the passengers they finally flew away.

The next day the sea was much more turbulent, the rolling and rocking of the ship seemed to make everyone grip their hands over the rails and no one asked for sausages and cheese. Almost everyone except the captain and Guillaume were throwing up over the side. Then they arrived at the port of Palermo where Guillaume had to get off and find another ship taking him to Spain.

The ship he found the next day was getting ready to leave. Guillaume hopped aboard with his baggage and stood for a long time watching the island of Sicily slowly disappear.

Sardo came up on them after a few days. Guillaume slept on deck. He was used to it. Then the ship sailed for another four days to Palma de Mallorca, unloading more passengers and goods. And then straightaway made for Seville.

Guillaume was getting homesick by the time the city came into view after several days of traveling and he remembered the visuals. Now he could easily see the landscape on both sides of him and he remembered the scent of fresh turned earth. Guillaume mentally began to relax.

In Seville he heard lovely music playing in the early afternoon as he switched the ship to a flat-bottomed boat and sailed all the way to Cordoba on the Guadalquivir River. And then the waterwheel came into view, scooping up water into tiny clay buckets and delivering it to a long sluice for the water deprived fields.

Cordoba was hot and lazy in the late afternoon sun not yet up from its siesta.

Guillaume got off the boat and paid. Then he pulled off his goods and baggage.

He ordered a carriage put his things into it and told the man where he wanted to go rent a house. Amazingly by some strange coincidence he got the same house at the end of Doctor's street as he had before. He threw his bags and luggage on the floor and went out to get something to eat.

The next morning Guillaume tried to find Zara. But he wasn't successful. Nor could he contact Jacques. So he hired a carriage to take him to Madinat Al-Zahra, the City of Zahra, the caliph's palace, where he used to have an apartment and a job.

After paying the carriage driver, he went around the back of the palace saw the floating silk banners trailing on seemingly eternal breezes, cool to the touch. As he stepped up on the marble floors he saw the announcer, who asked him who he was and what was his business here. Guillaume told the man and he marked it down in his large book. The announcer turned around and whispered something into the ear of a boy standing nearby. The boy took off running and a few minutes later the captain of the guard – smiling as always – walked boldly into the room.

"Guillaume de la Puy en Valley," he said.

Guillaume smiled at the captain and they hugged each other. A minute later something small tumbled and cartwheeled into this court. It was another of Guillaume's friends, the midget.

"Did you like that, I've been working on that entrance for over a month!" said the midget.

"Ibn Imran, court jester by trade, how have you been my little imp?" said Guillaume picking him up.

The captain laughed loudly.

"And you still stink like dead fish to high heaven!" said the midget.

The captain guided Guillaume to the apartments for unannounced guests with the jester coming along.

Guillaume began telling them his experiences about going home on a ship and the unexpected adventures that followed.

Caliph, Hakam II suddenly knocked on the door and the men presently excused themselves.

"Guillaume, how are you?" asked the caliph.

"I'm fine and how about you, Hakam?"

"Oh, I'm all right. We shall have to just call the nobles together and hear about all your adventures. How about Friday?"

"May I have my rooms back?"

"Your rooms are just as you left them last, Guillaume."

"Wonderful."

At that they both burst out laughing. It was almost like old-times, perhaps friendlier and relaxed now that each did not have anything to prove to the other.

Guillaume went to his old rooms. He found the cork put it in the bottom of the polished stone tub and turned on the water. Then he proceeded to get undressed. In came Ibn Imran who lit some incense. Guillaume got in the bath and relaxed. The imp had some new clothes ready for him to wear, doctor's clothes, as he would again be given that rank as well as pharmacologist, which they suspected Guillaume had trained for. The elevated rank of physician gave a man a grey stripe, and a pharmacologist gave him a cinnamon colored one, which elevated him to senior physician.

Guillaume smiled and sank deeper into the soapy water, it felt so good and promptly he fell asleep. The imp understood and quietly walked out of the room.

Guillaume woke up several hours later freezing and in the dark. Pulling the cork plug and grabbing a towel he stepped out of the bath and stood on a toweled floor. Rubbing the last of the water off he sat down and began getting dressed again in his new clothes. Then he went out to get a light from a passing stranger. Guillaume sat thinking about how he would get in touch with Zara if she were still alive.

The next morning Rabi came by knocking gently at his door.

"Rabi, how are you?"

"Well, I still have my old job, but I am almost eight years older. As you see, an old man."

"No you're not," protested Guillaume.

"You look well enough. So you journeyed on did you?"

"Yes, Rabi, I did. I can tell you many strange things and on Friday evening the Nobles are going to have a meeting in which I'm invited to speak. Will you come?"

"I will."

"Fine. Thanks. By the way, do you know how I might find Zara and my brother, Jacques?"

"Oh, sure, she's living in a business section of Cordoba, her address is…"

"You've kept in contact with her?"

"Of course. If you remember that letter I delivered for you from China as well as a letter for Jacques. Oh, yes, I knew of your interest and that kept me in touch with them. But Jacques might take a little longer, as there is no postal service either to or from his sanctuary. However, once a month…"

"Once a month he comes in town on his wagon to gather supplies, yes I know."

"Well, perhaps, with both of us trying to find him, we'll get lucky."

"All right, good night, my friend."

"Good night to you."

Guillaume was really glad Rabi had come by.

The following day Guillaume took a carriage to the ranch where he kept his horse Gift, which had been let out to those who would pay the stud fees. His horse remembered him instantly. The old man in charge came out and greeted Guillaume. His wife had died and he not getting married again. The stud fees were enough to keep him and the ranch and his horse going.

All this went down gladly for the old man as Guillaume put a harness on Gift, then a light blanket and saddle got up on Gift and turning the horse around he went off at a canter which he soon turned into a gallop when he let the horse go.

Then he rode on the horse into the business district, where it took him but a few minutes to find Zara's Singing & Dancing School. Guillaume got off his horse and went inside where Zara was conducting lessons for her students. She nearly fainted when she saw him, but had the sense to dismiss her girls.

"Guillaume!" she said.

"Zara."

"I thought you were dead!"

"I was until I saw you!"

She fell into his arms, crying and kissing him and he laughed and picked her up and taking her outside and put her up on Gift, the horse, then he swung on the back of his horse.

"Oh, I almost forgot! You've got to turn around and go back to the school, there is something I want to show you."

"Can't it wait?"

They turned around and walked the horse back. And so Guillaume stroked her hair in the sunlight while she tried to dry her happy tears.

She slid off the horse, told Guillaume to wait, and ran inside.

"All right Guillaume you can come in now."

Guillaume was in a very good mood, swung over the side of Gift and went slowly inside where he saw Zara standing up looking at him and something began moving out of her shadow. A little girl in a red dress, who looked very much like Zara, stepped aside and looked at Guillaume.

"I've been waiting for you for so long, you see this is the present I have for you, Guillaume."

Immediately Guillaume knew this was his child. It was a feeling he got, and a deep attachment that overcame him. He went over to her, got down on his knees and quietly addressed the girl: "Would you like to see my big white horse, Gift, he's just outside."

The young girl's face lit up and she nodded looking at him shy with half a smile.

"All right, sweetheart, let your mother and I take you to him."

The last of the girls were on their way out the back door and locked it. And Zara locked the front door while the little girl in the arms of Guillaume met Gift who snorted and smelled the girl nodding his large head several times.

"What is her name, Zara?"

"Olivia."

Then Guillaume jumped up on the horse and he grasped Zara's hands and pulled her up and then he said: "Come on Olivia, grab my hand."

And he pulled Olivia up in front of Zara."

Guillaume turned Gift into the sunlight and slowly made their way home toward Zara's place. It turned out that Rabi didn't have the story right. Zara didn't live in the business area, but actually lived out in the country. There was plenty of peace and quiet. And there was a barn next door to her cottage, where Guillaume could leave his horse and saddle. Then he went into Zara's home and looked around.

"This is a nice place, Zara."

"We think it is."

At first Guillaume hardly knew what to say to an eight year old child and the girl's shyness also made her back off a little. So, over the course of a long delicious dinner, Guillaume began talking about his experiences, he took off his shirt and showed the two of them his scars, which nearly made Zara cry again.

He spoke in detail about his journeys and adventures. Then it was Olivia's time for bed. Guillaume helped Zara clean up the kitchen.

He put his arms around her and asked her if she wanted to go to bed with him, and she became shy and so he picked the living room to sleep in.

The next morning Guillaume took them on his horse back to Zara's school, telling her that he had to find his brother and he would be back in the evening.

In the previous night, Zara had told him how Jacques would be coming to town the next day. She had seen him a few weeks earlier, and Jacques told her he would. They were planning to meet, and told Guillaume to wait by the meet market.

So Guillaume stood by the entrance to the fresh meat market. He wondered if Jacques had changed much, if he would recognize him, and he wondered if she shouldn't have asked Zara the night before instead of letting his pride get in the way.

After a while, Jacques came in but didn't see Guillaume, who stepped out of the shadows and spoke Jacques' name out loud.

Jacques turned around.

"Guillaume!"

And they hugged one another.

"I just got in a few days ago, Zara told me how to find you."

"Oh, I'm so very happy to see you," said his brother.

"Me too," replied Guillaume. "It has been a long time."

"Well, let's go and catch up, but first I'll have to get this meat to the market, even though its been cured it needs a dark and cool place for it to sit for a while. Where are you staying now-a-days?"

"In Doctor's Street where we had our home, don't you remember?"

"Oh, yes, of course, I remember."

"Let me finish up here, and I will come meet you," said Jacques, smiling and happy.

"Alright," replied Guillaume.

They hugged again.

Guillaume hopped up on Gift, and went off toward Doctor's Street. When he got home he began putting his things away. The dishes he put away first then clothing and then his journal and all his writings including the Arabic/Chinese dictionary of plant names and their uses.

He sat there for a good hour, and thought about all that he had been through since the last time he was there. All the places he visited, all the people he had met, and all the crazy experiences he has had.

He knew he had grown as a person, and he knew this was better for him both as a person and as a doctor. He thought about France, and the monks, and that monastery, all of it. Now he was a father, living in southern Spain, but there was more happiness here than he knew anywhere else.

Zara, he thought, and he smiled.

Later, he heard Jacques come up and went out to help him. Jacques came in bearing a nearly mature plant and placed it on Guillaume's desk.

"I don't believe I've ever seen this plant before," said Guillaume, "I think, no. My knowledge over the years may be a bit fuzzy as I haven't kept up with it."

"This plant is called Hindiba," explained Jacques. "It has just come from the East and it is supposed to heal cancerous growth," he added. "But it has many strengths, how good I don't know. It may very well replace some of your plant drugs, I guess we'll see."

"Well, thank you Jacques, you're a very kind man."

"We had to get out of Cordoba because the religious authorities were persecuting us, and, you were gone," said Jacques sarcastically.

Then Jacques began relating how a few years ago he had gone back home to Le Puy and visited his mother for his father had died a year before. His oldest brother had been taking very good care of her and the jewels which Guillaume and Jacques had given them placed his family up without worry.

"There are also some work papers which go with this Hindiba plant. The person who brought the plant here from Baghdad put it in his saddlebags, in a book, to keep it from the authorities, then watered it after taking it out, which is why it is still alive. The man who brought it was a friend of mine. We'll have to take it through its cycles to orient it to our climate."

"I'll have to go over these papers tonight and see what we've got, see how strong this plant is. Oh, there is one of your drawings in here, very good."

"You know, Guillaume, we were all of us wondering if you had died, then your letters arrived and told us where you were and that you were still alive, but not when you were going to return home."

"Where I was you mostly couldn't mail letters, I'm sorry about the lack of communication."

"Well, it's all over now, and I'm very glad to see you again."

"Won't you come next Friday to the meeting of Nobles when I tell my story?"

"Yes, I can, I'd like to hear that."

Jacques told his brother about his new life, his spiritual new life. He had met a mystical Muslim, and he was now a Sufi after some years of learning. He told his brother how it changed his life. He had gone through many experiences, or *hal*, and saw a different kind of life and was living a different way.

"I have to admit you look better than when I left," said Guillaume, smiling at his brother. "You look happier, and you look healthier, it's not easy to explain."

Jacques thanked his brother, and told him more about his life. Guillaume listened to his brother, and was fascinated by his new way of life.

He had missed so much.

Guillaume settled down into the life he'd had always longed for. The next day he realized that he hadn't fed Gift all night. So he took his books and put on the bridal and

371

saddle and with his books left for the palace. When he got there Guillaume asked the man in charge of the horses to take good care of his horse and feed him immediately. Then he brought in the books he'd written and gave an attendant the dictionary and told him the names of those who would benefit from it.

In half an hour, the chief physician came in with his book and said, "This book is kind of fantastic, did you do it all by yourself?"

"No, no, I had excellent help from a Chinese pharmacologist, as well as a doctor."

Hakam wanted Guillaume to take over the administration of the new pharmacology clinics. Three days at each with one day off each week. The only difference he could see was that people at the palace were required to pay for their medicines while those in town were not.

And Guillaume thought that that idea was fine with him. He was finally settling down now that he resumed his job, but as chief pharmacologist and as a staff physician, which was a promotion for him.

The Friday night lecture turned out well, all the nobles were there and all of Guillaume's friends. They all voted to give Guillaume another coat of honor. Very few people had ever gone, where Guillaume went and lived long enough to tell their tales.

In spring the poppies grew, opening their red petals and in the fields there was red everywhere. Guillaume was working again and felt better both by working with friends doing the job he loved and in a place where the freshest news was brought out from riders coming in from all parts of Andalusia.

Then summer came, heating up everything and making everyone enjoy the trees and large bushes for the shade they provided.

In late August and September there was time for everything. It seemed as if the world worked slower and slower until the coming of the rains.

In the court there was always music, in fact a twenty-four hour kind, a different hour of music for each different hour in the day played by very splendid musicians. It provided Guillaume with the most refined pleasure he could think of. Sitting and letting his mind drift with the music was an enormous pleasure.

He wondered how long this would last.

That night Guillaume went home and told Zara and Olivia about how his experiment had been going. When Olivia fell asleep and both he and Zara were tired he put the little girl into her bed. Then he took Zara by the hand into their bedroom and they made love.

The following morning Guillaume asked Zara for her hand in matrimony and she said: "Yes."

She clasped her arms around his neck and kissed him deeply.

A week later they were married in the Mozarabic church. Olivia was smiling all day long, though she did not understand the meaning of marriage. Some members of the nobles, including friends were there. Guillaume and Zara danced out of the Church and into the waiting carriage.

At some point Guillaume began thinking about visiting home as Jacques had done. And so he, Zara, and Olivia all made ready to leave by ship.

All was well in his world.

Author

Michael Arno Bender (1938 - 2015) was born in Oregon, lived in California before marrying and settling in Idaho. He had studied history and philosophy, and was in the military where he learned Russian and Chinese. Michael had a life long interest in Spain, especially in Andalusia where Judaism, Christianity, and Islam interacted over the 800 years that the Arabs were there. This is his second book.

www.ingramcontent.com/pod-product-compliance
Lightning Source LLC
Chambersburg PA
CBHW020837020726
47497CB00005B/1140